Conrad Richter *has written*

>*The Sea of Grass* (1937)
>
>*The Free Man* (1943)
>
>*Always Young and Fair* (1947)
>
>*The Trees* (1940) WHICH IS CONTINUED IN
>
>*The Fields* (1946) AND
>
>*The Town* (1950)
>
>*The Light in the Forest* (1953)
>
>*The Mountain on the Desert* (1955)
>
>*The Lady* (1957)
>
>*The Waters of Kronos* (1960)
>
>*A Simple Honorable Man* (1962)
>
>*The Grandfathers* (1964)
>
>*A Country of Strangers* (1966)
>
>*The Awakening Hand* (1966)

AND A VOLUME OF SHORT STORIES
Early Americana (1936)

THESE ARE BORZOI BOOKS, PUBLISHED BY
Alfred A. Knopf

THE SEA OF GRASS

THE

SEA OF

GRASS

BY

CONRAD RICHTER

ALFRED A KNOPF : *NEW YORK* : 1967

THIS IS A BORZOI BOOK,
PUBLISHED BY ALFRED A. KNOPF, INC.

PUBLISHED FEBRUARY 8, 1937
REPRINTED TWELVE TIMES
FOURTEENTH PRINTING, JANUARY 1967

Contents

10

PART I

Lutie

i

THAT lusty pioneer blood is tamed now, broken and gelded like the wild horse and the frontier settlement. And I think that I shall never see it flowing through human veins again as it did in my Uncle Jim Brewton riding a lathered horse across his shaggy range or standing in his massive ranch house, bare of furniture as a garret, and holding together his empire of grass and cattle by the fire in his eyes.

His rude empire is dead and quartered today

like a steer on the meat-block, but I still lie in bed at night and see it tossing, pitching, leaping in the golden sunlight of more than fifty years ago, sweeping up to his very door, stretching a hundred and twenty miles north and south along the river, and rolling as far into the sunset as stock could roam — a ranch larger than Massachusetts with Connecticut thrown in, his fabulous herds of Texas cattle sprinkled like grains of cinnamon across the horizons, his name a legend even then, his brand familiar as the A B C's in every packing-house, and his word the law, not dead sentences in a book, but a moving finger writing on a cottonwood tree where all who rode could very plainly read.

I can see his bedroom, just a bunk in the corner, with a fancy horsehair bridle and ropes on the wall, and a brown buckskin partly cut away in strips for whang leather. And I can see his huge parlor, without rugs or furniture, piled to the pine rafters with white sacks of flour and burlapped hills of sugar and green coffee, and wooden buttes of boxed to- bacco, dried fruits, and canned tomatoes, just the provisions for his hundred hands and everyone else who passed that way, rancher or cowboy, settler or prospector, Mexican, Indian, or outlaw, all wel- come at his table.

But what moves across my eye unforgettably is

his spring roundup when six or seven wagons working back from the Arizona line reached the head-
quarters range with a vast, almost mythical herd
the like of which will never be seen in this country
again. Farther than the eye could strain through
the dust, the grass was colored with milling cattle,
while bulls rode and fought, and cows and calves
bawled, and countless horns clacked, and sixty or
seventy of us kept saddling fresh mounts and
galloping here and there in a stirring, daylong
excitement.

The free wild life we lived on that shaggy prairie
was to me the life of the gods. And that there should
be anyone who would not love it as we did, who
should even hate it passionately and secretly, and
yet the memory of whose delicate presence in that
violent land still stirs me with emotion after fifty
years, had not occurred to me then. But I was only
a boy whose face had never known a razor, in a
pair of California britches turned up to let my
boots into the stirrups, that early fall day I rode
with rebellious young back to Salt Fork to be
shipped off to Missouri to school before my uncle
would fetch back to the ranch the scarcest article
in the territory, a woman, the one we had never
seen, who was coming all the way from St. Louis
to marry him.

At the edge of town I scowled at an encampment
of settlers' tents and wagons, the largest I remembered. They seemed to be waiting for something.
Then I rode up to the hotel and heard someone say
that the telegraph line was open after having been
cut again by Indians in the Raton.

" I'm going to let it to you, Hal, to see the
Colonel gets this," the red-faced station agent told
me mysteriously.

He handed me a sheet of unfolded gray paper,
the writing in pencil and dated at St. Louis nearly
a week before. It was, I think, the first telegram I
had ever seen and for a moment I had the impression that the paper itself had come in some up-to-
date manner over the telegraph wire and that the
execrable writing was that of this woman who had
signed it Lutie and who said with love that she was
not stopping off in Denver as she had planned but
would arrive in Salt Fork on a morning I knew
was tomorrow.

I had not seen my uncle for more than two weeks,
and with the telegram unpleasant as a perfumed
handkerchief in my pocket, I rode down to the
shipping corrals, half expecting to see his herd of
fall beef steers come sweeping down off the sand
hills into town like the Rio Grande running bank-
full after the summer rains, washing across the

tracks, flooding the stock-pens and overflowing along the river-bank from where, until shipped, they would fill the town night and day with their bawling.

But no Cross B steers were there and neither was my uncle, and I went to the dim adobe courtroom where they were outrageously trying two of our hands for shooting at and running off a nester. I couldn't get any nearer than the door. But from there I could hear the oratorical voice of the young district attorney, lately from the East and close to the President, bitterly assailing the high-handed methods on my uncle's vast range and promising new justice for emigrants in all his district from the Rio Grande to the Arizona line.

When the trial adjourned until morning, I pushed myself between groups of soberly talking men to Henry McCurtin, my uncle's lawyer, a ponderous man, who read the telegram over his great drooping dun mustaches.

"I haven't seen the Colonel since the trial opened," he rumbled. "I reckon, son, you better meet this woman tomorrow yourself."

For a long time I lay awake that night in the cavernous Bridal Chamber of the Exchange House, the corner room always reserved for my uncle when he came to town, feeling my hate for this woman

who was banishing me to Missouri, and thinking
that I had never known the town quite so swarming
with men, the livery stable and wagon yards so
choked with horses, or the night so deafening with
the clatter of pianos and scream of fiddles pouring
from open dance-hall windows; with the steady
undertone of clinking glasses from half a score of
saloons; and men and sporting women talking,
laughing, and yelling boisterous songs that paused
only for the sudden rap of the six-shooter.

But through it all I could hear, like the wild,
unceasing heartbeat of this frontier town, the
sound of marching boots on the wooden sidewalk,
pounding the planks from bar to bar. And I knew
that not all these men, drawn from a hundred and
two hundred remote miles, had come to ship beef.
It was the trial, this new young district attorney
from the East, challenging the power of my uncle
and other big cattlemen, that had drawn them. And
sitting up in that enormous bed I could see through
the long window the distant white tents and sheeted
wagons of the emigrants' camp glinting like the wet
and treacherous quicksands of the Puerco.

When I awoke in the morning, I found to my
regret that I had slept through another shooting.
On the way to the depot I saw the dead man's oxen
still hitched to his wagon, ten or twelve of them

lying down patiently in the yoke, chewing their cud, while the stranger who had done it swung a slow pendulum on the railroad's wooden water-tower, his boots already pulled off by some low wretch and the water dripping over him, his head to one side and one leg curiously longer than the other as if he were trying to reach the ground.

He was cut down by the sheriff under the indignant direction of the new district attorney and laid temporarily under a wagon sheet in the freight house. But as soon as the officers had disappeared into the courthouse, some of the dead teamster's friends dragged him out again just as I faintly heard a bell ringing and hand-brakes screeching from every open platform. I stayed to watch them take a rope from somebody's saddle and pull him up again. And when I turned, the train from St. Louis was long in, with its short coaches coated with the dust of the Great Plains.

Up until now I expected that at the last moment my uncle would surely appear. But he wasn't there, and I cast about harshly in my mind what I should say to this woman and how I might recognize her. In the territory my uncle attended strictly to business, riding the range as hard as any of his hands. But in Kansas City, where he went regularly to sell his cattle, people said that he swung a wide

loop and once when a prominent commission man
he much disliked had solicited him too far for his
business, even inviting him to a very elite party,
my uncle had forever silenced him by coming in
great style with a notorious and lavishly dressed
sporting woman on his arm.

And now I looked for a woman bold and painted
like Ready Money Kate from St. Louis, whom I
had often seen sailing up and down the wooden
sidewalks of Salt Fork in vivid silks with parasol
to match and, when she crossed the dusty street,
with plenty of red and white striped stocking showing.

All I saw was a lady standing by the car steps
and behind her a respectful, bearded brakeman
holding a pair of valises. Her face was hidden behind a heavy brown veil, but there was something
unforgettable in the slender way she stood there, in
a suit of unmistakable quality and tailoring, gloves
and a plumed hat, a fragile feminine figure, alone
and unmet, stared at by blanketed Indians,
Mongol-like Mexicans, and shaggy white men with
cartridge belts and with spur rowels coarse as cart-
wheels, and over their heads on the water-tank
the dead man still swinging.

A loafer in a buckskin shirt with all the beading
long since lost said something and pointed to me,

and I saw her move toward me. She did not speak until she was so close I could smell the fragrance of violets about her and could see the liquid of her eyes through the veil. Then she lifted it from her face, and although I was only a boy, I felt that quickening emotion she was always to arouse in me until the last time I should see her.

" So this is Hal? " she said softly, and kissed me, and I stood there young and rigid with my face burning in front of everyone. But if she saw it, she gave no sign. With the dead man slowly turning in front of her, she went on chatting to me in slightly incoherent but charming fashion, saying the gayest of things, that required little or none of my tongue-tied answers, all the while her delicate forehead shutting out the water-tank and that ring of staring loafers as completely as if she stood alone with me in my uncle's ranch house. And I realized that here was a finer-fibered creature than any my long black hair and rope-calloused hands had known.

When I stammered that her telegram had come only last evening and that I hadn't been able to deliver it to my uncle as yet, she took my arm with alive intimacy.

" We'll find him together, Hal," she said confidently.

" He'll come to the hotel, if you'll wait there,"
I told her.

" The bags can go to the hotel, but not I, Hal,"
she answered. " I've been shut up in a train for
days and days. I want to walk. Miles and miles,
until we find him."

Very stiffly and thinking these St. Louis ladies a
little mad, I guided her through the deep dust
strewn with horns and bones and the forelegs of
sheep, between wagon hubs and saddle-pony heels,
until we were up on the wooden sidewalk, where I
took care to steer her away from the direction of the
courthouse. But I couldn't avoid the wagon of the
dead freighter, with boys climbing a wheel to stare
at what we both could plainly see, a long figure lying on his back, with his red beard still sticking up
defiantly from under the blue bandanna across his
face. But Lutie Cameron's chatting never stopped.
Only her soft live arm tightened in mine like a doe-
skin band.

I had the pride common in the territory that
going about on foot was the mark of a hoeman and
close to disgrace. And I was glad when the boardwalk came to an end. But Lutie Cameron had
pinned her veil back now; her delicate face was
thrown up and there was no stopping her. On and
on we went past a few scattered Mexican houses and

up the sloping sand hills, where she exclaimed over
the common yerba de vibora still in blossom and
pinned a yellow spray of it gayly across her coat.

But when we reached the top of the escarpment
and, suddenly like coming on the ocean unaware,
there in front of us stretched the vast, brown,
empty plain, dipping and pitching endlessly like
a parched sea, she stopped as if she had run into
barbed wire. I tried to point out a remote, nearly
indistinguishable cloud shadow that marked the
general location of the distant ranch house, but she
didn't seem to hear me, chatting almost breathlessly about a traveling acquaintance on the Pull-
man palace car on her way to join her husband at
Fort Ewing, all the while striking out for the white
village of tents and covered wagons of the emigrants' camp near by, where life was busily going on.

She waved brightly to a score or more of children
tumbling, rolling, and shouting over the ground,
and bowed charmingly to tired-looking women in
sunbonnets who had been sewing and knitting on
a circle of wagon seats and rockers set on the grass
and who stood up now to receive her as some great
lady who had deigned to visit their humble abode.

When they told her they had come all the way
from her own Missouri and hoped to settle far out

on this very plain, something came into her eyes
that I hadn't seen there before. She sparkled to
grandmothers in knitted caps and wrinkled as Indians, swung a gurgling baby high in the air, and
ran and shouted with the children who had clustered around her. And she climbed up into one of
the wagons fitted up as a cabin with stove-pipe
pushing out of the canvas, where, as I stood stiff
and disapproving, I could hear her complimenting
the delighted owners on what she found.

" If you see Colonel Brewton," she said gayly
before she left, " tell him we've been looking for
him everywhere."

I was conscious of a shadow instantly falling
over the camp. Even the children seemed to freeze
at the sound of my uncle's name.

" I reckon you'll find him at court today,
ma'am," a gaunt Missourian answered after a
moment.

Lutie Cameron said nothing until we were a
quarter-mile away.

" Why did they look at us so queerly, Hal? And
why didn't you tell me we might find him at court? "

" We couldn't get in anyhow," I answered sul-
lenly.

And when we reached the square, I could see at
the courthouse a little crowd of men packed half-

way across the boardwalk to the hitching-rack. I
would have gone on to the Exchange House, but
she stopped and lifted her head in that gesture I
already knew so well, a slight feminine figure
against the rude backs of a score of men.

" May we pass, please? " She spoke clearly, and
to my surprise that gentle lady's voice of hers
turned rough men about and tumbled off their hats
as if a bullet had whipped them. A narrow but unmistakable aisle opened in front of us, and presently I found myself inside, with Blackjack Kerns,
a rustler and outlaw, rising like a jack-in-the-box
to give the lady his seat, and others on the bench
moving over to make a few inches of room for me.

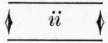

ii

THE SALT FORK COUNTY court was stuffed and smelly as a stock corral at shipping time, a dingy adobe room with earthen floor and small Mexican windows darkened by men sitting on the deep ledges so that it seemed as if we had entered a kind of rude twilight.

" Is he here, Hal? " Lutie Cameron whispered to me through her veil.

16

But even before my eyes grew accustomed to the dimness, I knew by the atmosphere that my uncle wasn't there.

"The jury's comin' in," a cowhand from the Three V's muttered behind me.

I saw now that the jury box of worn and whittled pine benches was empty. Then I heard a stir at the doorway behind us and presently I thought I could feel a wave of restrained excitement rising in the rear of the room and passing from bench to bench until beyond the railing I saw our two accused cowhands twist in their seats and Henry McCurtin turn like a mountain suddenly come to life.

I felt my arm brushed by Lutie Cameron's gloved fingers.

"What is it, Hal?" she whispered.

Then I saw by her veiled eyes that she glimpsed something and, turning my head, I saw it, too, moving erect and towering down the crowded aisle along the wall, a familiar, proud, almost insolent figure in a long gray broadcloth coat with tails and bulging on the side toward us with what I knew was a holster capped with ivory handles, his coal-black eyebrows and mustache white with alkali dust, and in the abrupt quiet of the room the fall of his boot-heels like the shots of a pistol.

Since that day I have been in many a courtroom,
but never any so quickly transformed from a dingy
room to one kindled and illuminated by the light-
ning-flash of one man's vitality and power, so that
today I can still see it as in the strongest sunshine,
the dusty colors of the American flag on the whitewashed wall over the judge's pine bench, and beneath his parted black robe the gold links of his
watch-chain, heavy enough for carriage traces, on
the court rail a pair of buckled spurs swinging, and
that fearless, moving figure of my uncle like some
rude territorial czar.

Then I saw that those pitchfork eyes which
missed nothing had found us. Deliberately, with
scarcely a change in him, he was crossing to our
aisle, the men on the bench he chose to pass by
scattering for the moment like sheep in front of
him. And presently he stood there beside us with
bared head and a kind of mellowed dignity, press-
ing Lutie Cameron's hand, asking her health and
welfare in quiet solicitude, his great lusty face
gently warmed like the sunlight on a weathered
cliff.

Saying he would join us later, he straightened,
his black glance swept those close by who had been
listening, and he moved majestically on, passing
inside the privileged railing where Henry McCur-

tin stood up in massive welcome and the two accused cowhands grinned and the sheriff hastily
brought him the bailiff's chair, while the district
clerk with a pen riding one ear stared respectfully
and Judge White, peering as always with a glum
and imperturbable face over his pine bench, broke
into a friendly smile and his head bobbed in cere-
monious greeting.

Only one man inside of the railing showed him
no deference, and I watched Brice Chamberlain,
the young district attorney appointed by the President, standing there tall and impressive, his plain
sack coat buttoned close to his white collar, his
brows frowning formidably, and his thick blond
hair sweeping back in a kind of masterful and
handsome disapproval.

" What's the case about, Hal? " Lutie Cameron
whispered. " And who is the scowling gentleman? "

I didn't answer. The faded blue door beyond the
railing had opened and men were starting to drift
through, in single file, slouching Americans in sagging unbuttoned vests and slightly pompous Mexicans in leather chalecos, one after the other pulling
off his hat as he entered, boots shuffling on the
adobe floor.

Behind me a voice whispered loudly that for any
other man except Jim Brewton the jury would

have stayed out with their verdict until they had had their dinner on the county. Then I heard leathery Eli Jones, the jury foreman, answering Judge White's questions.

"We find," he drawled, "that Andy Boggs was shot at and run off the place he wanted to file on, by unknown parties."

I saw the strict face of the judge redden as if over some impropriety.

"That's no verdict!" he reminded sharply. "The two defendants —"

"Oh, hell, they're not guilty," Eli waved.

I wanted to give the Apache war-whoop while behind me a row of cowhands stamped their boots and jingled their spurs until Judge White pounded his pine bench in anger. Then he demanded the formal written verdict of the grinning jury foreman and adjourned court.

"Is that the verdict you wanted, Hal?" Lutie Cameron asked eagerly, but I saw that her eyes were not on me or our freed cowhands; rather on the tall young district attorney, who had winced as if thrown by a horse.

Another moment and she had urged me up from our bench. With her arm in mine, she swept up the aisle, chatting with animation at every step, and through the railing, where she stopped beside my uncle, slipping her free arm delicately through his, just as I saw Brice Chamberlain get himself in hand and stiffly congratulate Henry McCurtin.

Then the defeated young district attorney turned to my uncle.

"May I ask a few questions that I had no opportunity for during the trial, Colonel Brewton?"

His manner was courteous, but there was a faintly challenging ring in his voice and a blue fire in his eyes that kindled the silent attention of those of us standing inside of the railing. He went on without waiting for assent:

"Is it true, Colonel Brewton, that your range runs a hundred miles or more north and south, and west nearly to the Arizona line?"

My uncle merely inclined his head.

"Is it true," Chamberlain went on, his voice suddenly rising, "that of this vast country you control, you actually own only a few scattered water-holes that have been filed on either in your name or those of your men? And that by far the greater part still belongs to the government?"

"Legally, yes," my uncle conceded.

"Is it true, then," Chamberlain concluded, his voice gathering force and indignation, "that this million or more of acres still belonging to the government is the same land that Andrew Boggs, who only wanted a mere hundred and sixty acres for a homestead, was run off from and severely wounded by unknown parties?"

"No," my uncle said quietly but with great firmness and power. "He was not run off because he wanted to settle those hundred and sixty acres but because of what he wanted to do with the land."

So intent had I been on the sparks beginning to fly between the flint and steel of these two men that I had almost forgotten where we were. Now I heard a strong murmur of approval and, looking around, I saw a press of cowhands and cattlemen against the railing.

Brice Chamberlain did not glance around. But something seemed to pass behind his brightly burning blue eyes. His manner changed. An appeal came into his face and voice, and standing there bent persuasively toward my uncle, even I for a moment thought him modest and almost likable.

"Let's forget about this case, Colonel Brewton. Andrew Boggs was only a single man and the court has disposed of him. Waiting at the edge of Salt Fork to see how this trial comes out are other settlers. Not single men, but with families, from babes at the breast to grandmothers. They have given up their homes in the East, driven their wagons more than a thousand miles across the

plains, and left their dead from the Mississippi to
the Rio Grande — all with the one purpose of
finding homes for themselves in this great territory." His voice grew eloquent with pleading.
" Now that you have won your case, Colonel Brewton, and can afford to show your sympathy and
charity, I want to ask in the names of these
families if you won't let them settle undisturbed on
a few acres out of the million or more of government land on your range? "

I saw Lutie Cameron's eyes, soft under her veil,
glance expectantly at my uncle. But he didn't see
her. He had thrown up his head like an unruly lead
steer smelling wolves or water.

" Chamberlain," he said, " I have sympathy for
the pioneer settler who came out here and risked his
life and family among the Indians. And I hope I
have a little charity for the nester who waited until
the country was safe and peaceable before he filed
a homestead on someone else's range who fought
for it. But — " and his voice began to ring in the
small hushed courtroom, " when that nester picks
country like my big vega, that's more than seven
thousand feet above the sea, when he wants to plow
it up to support his family where there isn't enough
rain for crops to grow, where he only kills the grass
that will grow, where he starves for water and feeds

his family by killing my beef and becomes a man
without respect to himself and a miserable menace
to the territory, then I have neither sympathy nor
charity!"

His eyes now were pitch-black, proud, insolent,
his great face written with power and almost dissolute ruthlessness. "And I want to say," he finished, "that if I know the temper of the citizens
who ran off that worthless nester, Boggs, they'll
keep running off every granger who tries to destroy
their range!"

For nearly a minute more the two men faced
each other, one older, rugged, utterly fearless; the
other young and white with emotion.

"They warned me," Brice Chamberlain said in
a low burning voice, "not to bring action against
you or your men. They told me there was no justice
here, that you dominated the country and would
never share your land with your less fortunate fel-
low men."

He turned on his heel and left, but all of us knew
this was not the end. I looked at Lutie Cameron.
She still hung on my uncle's arm, delicate, silent,
rigid, her eyes on the stunned little group of listening Missourians in the patched blue and striped
jumpers of farmers huddled there in the courtroom. And when she and my uncle went out to the

hotel for dinner, I saw her take the spray of bright yellow blossoms she had pinned so gayly across her coat and throw it away.

With my hat hot and uncomfortable in my hand, I waited as long as I dared that afternoon outside the ladies' parlor of the Exchange House. When I pushed in the door, I saw my uncle standing with dignity in front of the tall window. Beside him stood Lutie Cameron, her head thrown firmly up, her brown veil raised, her plumes at a high and gallant angle, making an unforgettable picture in that dark, cavernous room with a single shaft of sunshine pouring over her, while Judge White in a long black coat with broad silken lapels kept sternly clearing his throat and compressing his lips as he read the unfamiliar marriage service.

Her cheeks were dusted as if with flour when she turned, but nothing else betrayed her as Dr. Reid, who, I think, must have denied himself liquor all afternoon for the occasion, bowed like the Virginian he was, over her hand, and wished her happiness. And Henry McCurtin, in fresh linen unsullied by a single tobacco stain, asked her jovially through his dun mustaches how she had managed to rope such a shy war-horse.

She and my uncle took me to the depot, and the last thing I saw of Lutie Brewton, she was stand-

ing with one arm outstretched waving her handkerchief gayly after me, a gesture I coldly declined
to answer. But late that night when the train was
puffing through the dark New Mexican hills, I
kept thinking about her in that walled island of
ranch house on my lost sea of grass.

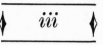

iii

I HAVE hated places in my life, but never any like that academy in Lexington where the woman who had waved me good-by so gayly had imprisoned me, with its brick walls and stone banisters still patched where grape-shot and Minie balls had torn through, with a winter of cold such as I had never known in the territory, with the sun not coming out for weeks at a time and a road of dirt and ashes

across the mile-wide Missouri frozen into curious
yellow ice.

And when spring came and the eaves dripped a
steady tattoo and strange birds cheeped in the
wet trees around the school, the ice went out of the
Missouri with a roar. And I went, too, between two
suns, as my uncle used to say of any man who disappeared. And late that afternoon I was in Kansas
City, trying to keep my chin up and my back stiff
and not to betray how bewildered I was in this cold
young city with wagons and carriages clattering in
every direction on the stone paving and no one paying me more attention than if I were a burro dozing
in the dusty streets of Old Town in Salt Fork. The
thought of those quiet, dusty streets sleeping in
the yellow sun made me more homesick for the territory than I have ever been in my life except for
a half-hour later when I reached the stockyards
and smelled cattle again and saw the familiar colors of longhorns and listened to Nicholas Masters
of the Masters Packing Company, the heavy flesh
of his face quivering like a kind of purple jelly
as he coughed and shook a fat finger at me and
sputtered that if he helped me run home, my uncle
would never sell him another trainload of steers.

But when I told him it had been the woman my
uncle had married and whom I hated that had

clapped me into this prison of a school, he stared
at me thoughtfully as a companion in distress. And
when I left, I had a pass and some money and had
given a sacred promise never to let this woman
know who it was had befriended me.

All the way out to the ranch on a Salt Fork horse
from Dagget's livery stable, with the range already greening up in the sloughs, with Canada
geese rising from the ponds and cutting the sky
like joined Apache lances, with calves kicking and
bucking in the spring sunshine and horses rubbing
off winter hair, I felt the bitterness grow in me for
the woman who would have kept me from all this.
And I planned coldly how I would treat her and
what curtness of speech she should hear from
me.

Riding up Nester Draw so she should not see
me coming, I cut across the rise and up to the rear
of the ranch house, where a strange Chinaman cook
eyed me suspiciously from the kitchen as I entered
by the back door. I scowled to see that there were
strange pine settees covered with Navajo blankets
in the wide hall. And glancing into the open door
of the huge storeroom, I saw with dull anger that
the familiar mountains of flour and coffee had vanished and the buttes of dried fruits gone, so that
I hardly knew the room with a Brussels carpet on

the floor and heavy dark red hangings at the windows and tufted horsehair chairs and sofa around
the walls and a square piano with legs curved and
lid polished as elegantly and offensively as the
piano at school.

It all had an inexpressibly depressing effect on
me, as if the old ranch house I had known and loved
was gone. And I stood there lonely, bitter, and
stiffening as a slender form appeared from the big
front bedroom in the dim hall. Oh, she looked a bit
thinner and paler, but her dark hair even here on
these remote plains was done up in the latest St.
Louis fashion; a spray of pink loco weed had been
pinned freshly across her basque and she still
moved with undiminished sparkle and aliveness.

Then she recognized me.

" Hal! " she almost screamed.

Her intense young arms hugged me as if she
had seen no one for weeks. And with her delicate
fragrance of violets about me like some sweet drug,
I felt the hate go out of me as the ice had gone out
of the Missouri at Lexington only a week or two
before.

Another moment and she was holding me at
arm's length, delightedly looking me over from
head to foot, squeezing my hand and laughingly
exclaiming what a manly boy I was on the way to

becoming, and chattering that she had not had a
visitor since day before yesterday and what a won-
derful winter she had spent here on the ranch in
this Western climate with blue sky and almost eter-
nal sunshine, and that my uncle was looking more
distinguished than ever, and had I seen the trees
she had coaxed the hands to plant for summer
shade; degrading work, my uncle had called it, that
men who rode a horse would never do.

But with nearly every word I observed in her
dark eyes the feverish brilliance of the first day I
had seen her. And the following year when I came
home a little older and taller, it still haunted her
eyes although the parlor hummed with company.
And I soon found out that scarcely a day was intended to pass without midday dinner guests or
overnight guests or guests to stay the week. And
most of them crocheted or embroidered, laughed or
sang, played charades or whist, and were agreeable
to almost anything except to ride out and visit
the roundup, which Lutie Brewton kept finding
charming excuses to miss.

There were, I remember, the sporting English
owners of the Bar 44 and the dancing officers from
Fort Ewing, the lively Falconers and important
Netherwoods, whose name Lutie Brewton loved to
trill over her tongue, the guests from Santa Fe and

Albuquerque, and Judge White and Brice Chamberlain on their respective rounds of the district court.

But if I expected my uncle to resent any of their coming, I was mistaken. He rode his range no less hard than before, and it must have seemed to him as it did to me a kind of miracle to step from dark night into a lighted house, from a hard saddle to a cushioned chair, to come from the cold, shaggy plain into warm curtained rooms with Lutie Brewton bare-armed in a silken gown and white candles burning around her as in a cathedral, with silver sparkling and stainless cloth shining and a mellow atmosphere of company talking and laughing around his table.

My uncle would bow with proud courtesy to everyone. But I heard him talk very little, preferring to sit there with a faint desert glow warming his weathered face, his insolent eyes softening a little as he watched or listened to his wife. No matter who came or how large the dinner, Lutie Brewton was the tireless pure flame burning in the center of it, her face flatteringly raised to listen, her talk a highly seasoned language of its own, her headlong treble laughter leading into general bursts of merriment, and her ringed fingers skimming over the white keys of the piano, with the soft light from the tall marble, brass, and china lamp golden on her dark hair.

She never stopped, not even for a moment. And when I watched her so alive on the black horsehair sofa, making ecstatic gestures with her white hands to the gentleman on either side of her, I had the curious feeling that she never slept, but, stimulated by congenial friends, could go on bubbling night and day.

Certainly she never stopped when she went to town with her fast team of bays to spend the night at the Netherwoods' or the Holdernesses', who were kin of Brice Chamberlain. Once or twice I drove her, and the moment we passed out through the dense wall of cottonwoods and tamarisks, she chatted incessantly, her sensitive face turned away from the wide sea of grass as if it were the plague, so that I swore she never saw the road runner racing with the carriage wheel or the antelope moving among the cattle. And I thought that at last I had begun to understand the reason for her wall of cottonwoods and tamarisks, which had not been planted for summer shade at all.

" She'll settle down once she has babies," I heard Mrs. Netherwood say fondly to Judge White the day of the Holman wedding, when she wore diamond dust in her hair.

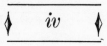

iv

THE BABIES came soon afterwards. One after the other I found them in the big front bedroom of the ranch house when I came home from school; the first, a fat gurgling girl with dark eyes and scarcely any hair to start with; the second, an unsmiling boy with the blackest of hair and eyes; and the third, a boy whose eyes were an unexpected bright blue, with hair so white and soft it turned and ruffled like a feather in my breath.

34

Yet neither I nor anyone else could see a change in Lutie Brewton. With her first baby in the cradle, I felt that out of respect I should call her Aunt Lutie, but she turned on me quickly.

"Don't you dare call me that, Hal!" she said and her eyes were black and flashing. " I shall never be old enough to be Auntie to anyone."

Black Hetty, who took care of the babies, showed the broad white of her teeth. But after the second child Lutie Brewton was still the same slender figure, alive, intense, her delicate white skin without a wrinkle. And with the third baby scarcely in his cradle, she danced eight out of ten square dances and waltzes with Brice Chamberlain as her partner in the huge English hall of the Bar 44.

He was at my uncle's ranch house now all too often to suit me, driving out as a rule with his dashing cousin, the young blond Mrs. Holderness, whether my uncle was home or not. The administration at Washington had long since changed and with it his and Judge White's appointments. And Brice Chamberlain had opened a law office on the dusty Salt Fork plaza next door to Gidding's dance hall, where he specialized in the settling of titles to the huge land grants for profit and the filing of homestead entries as a passion.

My uncle paid him little attention, while he

treated my uncle with unfailing politeness. But more than once when the latter wasn't looking, I caught Brice Chamberlain's blue eyes measuring him and seeming to say: " You're of the past generation now. Your time is soon over. We will run the world from now on, not you." And to Lutie he openly and eloquently boasted: " Civilization is moving west fast. It will be here soon. And when it comes, the fertile plains around this ranch house will be dotted with farms and schoolhouses."

I paid him no more attention than my uncle. But once when I coldly carried him an invitation to dinner, I saw his desk piled high with semi-transparent blueprint maps of township and correction lines and with stacks of letters from scores of land-hungry Easterners he had circularized, a sight that gave me an angry, disturbed feeling.

I was in college at St. Louis when the Washington administration changed again. Almost as I was leaving for home I read with satisfaction in the Salt Fork paper, printed in both English and Spanish, that Brice Chamberlain was closing up his office, turning all his legal matters over to Lawyer Archie Meade and going to establish residence in Denver, where he had been promised the appointment of United States district attorney. And two weeks later when I found him still in Salt

Fork, I scowled at his figure crossing the dusty plaza with that impressive long-legged stride, immaculately dressed as always with high-buttoned Eastern suit under an imposing silver-gray Western hat.

I turned to see Henry McCurtin, a little heavier and slower, his drooping dun mustaches a little grayer, standing there ponderously watching him from his inscrutable, deeply buried eyes.

" You glad as I am he's going? " I asked when we had shaken hands.

" I'm not so sure, Hal, not so sure. The town is full of rumors," he rumbled. Then, as if he had said too much, he turned massively away.

For the first time I became sensitive to things unsaid, that the waves of sand hills rolling toward the town held a stormy and faintly ominous look. And when I glanced back, I saw that the landlocked harbor of the square was taut and white with the crowded canvas of settlers' wagons from a dozen Eastern ports. And now I remembered all the small emigrant trains I had glimpsed from my train window across Kansas and through the Raton wherever the wagon trail lay in sight of the tracks.

And when I reached the ranch next day, I thought that I had never seen Lutie Brewton more brilliantly alive and restless. her cheeks flushed, her

eyes feverish, almost dazzling. All afternoon her
tongue poured out a stream of gay excitement,
one minute warm and frank and intimate as a sis-
ter, the next coaxing and teasing, while my small
cousins burrowed under my chair and climbed on
my shoulders and wore my new silver watch and
chain.

As a rule Lutie Brewton treated her children like
some gracious lady who had consented to be their
godmother. But tonight to my mild surprise she
told Black Hetty she would put them to bed herself. And with me standing in the doorway silent
at the picture they made, she poked grave, tender
fun at little Jimmy's skinny freckled legs and arms,
and called Sarah Beth's panty waist a corset, which
embarrassed her, and frowned with mock serious-
ness at the transparent white skin of Brock, whom,
she declared, God had intended to be a girl. And
all the while her facile white hands helped them to
slip off their garments and into their long muslin
nightgowns which covered their toes as they knelt
on the brown sheepskin.

But when we were back again in the parlor, I
saw her shudder, and I stared at her until she
turned on me like a white tigress.

"Why must you look at me like that, Hal? Am

I older? Am I sallow? What do you see? Have I pouches under my eyes? "

I lied to her that I had seen nothing, telling her the truth that she looked scarcely older than the day I had met her at the South Fork depot, and in a moment she had changed back to the sparkling person I knew. But during the night I thought I heard someone moving about the great front bedroom, and when I awoke as the sun heaved up red above the plain, the one who hadn't slept was still walking.

Except for a few minutes at breakfast and noonday dinner, I did not see her all day. I had planned to ride out to the roundup as was my custom, but something in her eyes withheld me. All afternoon I could hear her moving about mysteriously in her room. About six o'clock I was lying on my back on the slippery horsehair sofa, staring up at the heavy pine ceiling, when I heard the swish of skirts through the hall. And when I turned my head, she was standing there.

" You are almost a man now, Hal," she told me. " You've been to St. Louis and Kansas City, and you know the way of the world. And I think you'll understand when I tell you I'm going away."

Looking up from where I lay, the light in her

eyes seemed almost blinding. She went on a little
breathlessly:

"Run away, perhaps, is what you'd call it, Hal.
What people will call it. I'm running off. Leaving
your uncle for always. I'm going tomorrow morning, and I shan't be back."

I sat up stupefied. I had heard of occasional
women deserting their husbands, but for Lutie
Brewton to leave my uncle and her position in this
luxurious ranch house seemed unthinkable. I remembered he was still out at the roundup, which
on our range lasted from spring to summer, and she
must have read my thoughts in my eyes.

"Oh, I'm not running off behind his back, Hal,"
she said to me. "I told him nearly a month ago.
When the first emigrant wagons came to Salt Fork.
I told him I couldn't stand it another year. Not
running them off again and perhaps killing them
as they did that poor nester from Louisiana who
shot at them last year. He was white trash, but he
had a wife and six or seven children. Now, as far
as I am concerned, it's all settled — all but the
tearing out of a few roots and tendrils."

"But Jimmy and Brock and Sarah Beth?" I
stammered.

The first white hardness came into her face.

"I went over it and over it with him, Hal! A

thousand times, I think. You know your uncle. He thought he could hold me by holding the children. But nothing can stop me. My lawyer says I can't take them along. But I can fight for them after I'm away. Once we're settled. No jury, Hal, not even Mexicans, can keep three children from their mother."

Something between the lines of what she said troubled me.

" You're going away with somebody? " I heard myself saying coldly.

Unexpected warm color crept up into her faintly wilted cheeks, freshening them like petals, and almost at once she was like a flower rooted again in rich wet earth with that unaccountable power we call life flowing through her.

" If I never knew it before, Hal, I'd know now you had the same blood as your uncle. You ask the same questions. But I shan't tell you any more than I shall him. He's coming now. Don't go, Hal! " she begged quickly as I stiffened and rose. Her slender fingers gripped my arm. " You'll break the ice between us. And don't look so frightened for me, you poor boy! " Something shining and irrevocable came into her face. " I'm not dying and being stuffed into a coffin. I'm going where there's life, Hal. I'm going to balls and theaters and shaded

streets and up-to-date stores and where every day
people drive in the parks!"

I could hear hoofbeats now. Turning, I saw
through the deep windows my uncle riding toward
the ranch house, sitting erect as always in his saddle, his right arm held stiffly down against his
side with his thumb at the cantle edge as was his
custom, unchanged from army days. Presently
there was the sound of his boots and spurs through
the hall, and he was in the room. But, contrary to
what I feared, I had never seen him more quiet.

Lutie Brewton held up her face to be kissed as
always and chatted brightly to him of some of the
incidents I had told her of college, while my uncle
shook my hand and inquired if I had seen Nicholas
Masters as he had written me. There was a curious
absence of time and hurry, as if utterly nothing
had happened or was expected to happen. Only
when I glanced closely to see if Lutie had really
told me the truth did I feel the fine filaments of
strain in the air like those unseen currents that are
said to lift the hair of a wolf before an August
thunderclap.

"Supper's on the table, Miz Brewton," stoically
called Jeff Calder, the old chuck-wagon cook who
had long since followed the Chinaman in the ranch-
house kitchen.

I would have given a great deal that night to have avoided the dining-room and the massive silver. My uncle ate gravely while Lutie Brewton single-handed with almost desperate gayety kept conversation alive. But every moment I saw that she curbed her eyes from the windows.

The children had had their supper early tonight as was their custom, and now, with Black Hetty standing by, they were all astride the bare back of Old Cherry, scarcely taller than a pony. Jimmy sat in front; Sarah Beth, who was six or seven, behind him; and Brock to the rear, each holding to a share of the bridle reins. A strip of gunnysack as a blinder had been tied over the gentle old barefoot mare's eyes, and she stood motionless until Jimmy yelled and pulled it off, when she came to life and bobbed up and down until one happily shrieking youngster after the other was deposited on the grass.

I could not look at them myself tonight, and under my breath I muttered that as soon as it was dark I should saddle one of the night horses and ride to the camp at Cottonwood Springs, where I would stay till it was over. Then just before Lutie Brewton rose, she gave me one of her indecipherable glances.

"If I don't see you any more tonight, Hal," she

asked, " could you drive me to Salt Fork in the morning? "

My uncle had been sitting quietly on his chair, waiting for her signal to rise, the deferent courtesy he always had for her mellowing his face. Now his head was flung up in the gesture of a challenged wild stallion while his dark eyes flamed with sudden will and power.

" Hal will take your trunk in the buckboard," he told her proudly. " I'll drive you to the train myself."

" Thank you, Colonel Brewton," she said.

But I saw in an instant as she rose that an unusual pallor had swept her face. And when a few moments later I passed the length of the hall to the gallery, I saw her standing rigid in the huge front bedroom with her back toward a pair of ivory handles holstered in a heavy belt darkened by years of sweat and hanging on a high, brass harness hook out of reach of the children.

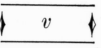

v

For a long time I lay awake that night in the bunk that had once been my uncle's, listening at intervals to the faint bawling of a calf for its mother in some dim, starlit cañada. And when I fell asleep I dreamed that something vaguely beautiful had gone out of this massive ranch house like the kernel of life out of a prairie seed, and all that remained was the brown shell of adobe walls staring from its empty sockets. And everywhere about the house in my dream, the sand was endlessly blowing, burying the print of the coyote and lizard, rattling in the vibora weed, drifting close to the ground like barren snow so that the whole earth seemed to be moving, a restless gray ghost of itself trying to find those full, lusty prairie breasts, fertile as a woman and flowing with milk and wild honey, that used to be.

At the first sound of morning I was up pulling on my clothes in the darkness and drinking coffee in the kitchen to escape the breakfast-table, and lending a hand in the starlight to the hitching of the teams. And when I came back to the long dark hall, I glimpsed in a candle-lighted room, framed like a picture by the heavy doorway, Lutie Brewton, suited, hatted, and one hand gloved, sitting with three sleepy youngsters in their nightgowns about her. And I heard her promising in that clear, delightful, fun-loving voice she always used to children, that she would see them all sooner than soon and would have a double present for each one that Black Hetty should say had been a little lady or gentleman.

Old Jeff helped me carry out her trunk to the sagging buckboard. And soon Lutie Brewton came, a slender, almost jaunty figure in the dim, blue-black light, answering the children's good-by before my uncle helped her up into the top buggy. Before the horses started, she answered again. And from somewhere down beyond the spring I heard her voice a last time, high and clear above the thud of hoofs and rattle of spokes, like some incredibly sweet and lingering bell.

Old Jeff had waited by one of the buckboard wheels, never saying a word, but I could hear him draw hard and furiously on his pipe until the sounds of the buggy grew faint on the night air. Still saying nothing, he moved grimly into the house while I climbed into the rig and my horses without urging followed those that had gone before.

To the newcomer in our Southwestern land it seems that the days are very much alike, the same blue sky and unchanging sunshine and endless heat waves rising from the plain. But after he is here a year he learns to distinguish nuances in the weather he would never have noticed under a more violent sky; that one day may be clear enough, and yet some time during the night, without benefit of rain or cloud, a mysterious desert influence sweeps the heavens. And the following morning there is air

clearer by half than yesterday, as if freshly rinsed
by storm and rain.

It was such a morning that I hauled Lutie
Brewton's trunk through the crystal air to Salt
Fork, with horses and buckboard moving at first
under the swinging lamp of the morning planet,
and then through a green, velvet twilight that was
half-way between stars and sun, and finally in the
early purple light that poured over the plain like
wine, until it seemed that with every breath I could
taste it, and even the stolid cattle feeding beside the
trail seemed to lift their heads to stare at it. And
when the sun shook the earth finally clear, I saw a
wave of antelope flowing inquisitively toward the
buggy far ahead, a wave rusty as with kelp, rising
and falling over the grassy swells and eventually
turning in alarm, so that a thousand white rumps,
whirled suddenly into view, were the breaking of
that wide prairie wave on some unseen reef of this
tossing upland sea.

Most of the way across the vegas I could have
reached out my hand and touched the fragrant
rows of bee balm starting to bloom on either side
of the trail. But all I could smell was the perfume
of violets rising from Lutie Brewton's trunk. And
all I could see now was a faint, distant column of

black smoke hanging in the sky, little more than a smudge in that illimitable air, yet already it threw a shadow over buckboard and trail.

The sun was a branding iron on the back of my neck when we came at last to the edge of the sand hills and I saw the cottonwoods standing already cool in shadow in the river valley below. My spent horses plowed the floury dust of the long street. And the red-faced station agent himself came bustling out to oversee the careful lifting of Lutie Brewton's trunk to the steel-protected baggage truck slatted like a buckboard and trundled like a barrow.

Not until then did I look up and see with relief that everything about the station was normal and everyday, the groups of passengers through the open door of the waiting-room, the loafers playing mumbletypeg on the plank platform, and out near the tracks a circle of friends surrounding Lutie Brewton, laughing and chattering as always, wishing her a pleasant visit to St. Louis and promising gay times when she returned. I could smell the calm unhurried redolence of ties lately simmering in the sun, could hear down in their whitewashed shipping pens the monotonous baas of a flock of lambs. And nearer, the white dust floated from a car of flour being unloaded in sacks to a dusty wagon.

Then I glimpsed Lawyers Henry McCurtin and
Archie Meade talking together in low, grave tones
beyond the baggage barrow, and was slowly conscious that all was not quite what it seemed. And
when I glanced around again, I was aware that the
loafers kept peering up stealthily from under their
brows, and a group of passengers whispered from
the waiting-room doorway.

And now I was sure that all those happy friends
were frantically playing a part and that they
really had no more belief that Lutie Brewton was
going to St. Louis than I had. And when I stumbled
by as if I noticed nothing, I saw that for all her gay
animation, her high lace collar was a pale branch
whipsawing in the pounding stream of blood at her
throat and that the veins on one of my uncle's hands
stood out like long-suppressed whipcords of blue
lightning.

I couldn't have gone now if I had wished. I could
see the grim bulge in my uncle's coat of gray
broadcloth and an untamed violence, like a prairie
fire rimmed with black smoke, flaring in his dark
eyes. Several loafers had risen to their feet licking
their lips. Following their eyes, I glimpsed up the
street the unmistakable tall figure of Brice Chamberlain in a new brown suit coming out of the Ex-

change House and pausing for a moment on the high stone steps, a Mexican behind him with a pair of gripsacks. Then both approaching figures were blotted out by the gray clot of rounded emigrant canvas.

PART II

The   Colonel

The Colonel

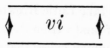

vi

THERE are pictures nearly dead in my memory now that I never thought I should forget: the curl of a yellow sand wave in the black malpais; the bend of grama grass in the June wind; and the glitter of mocking desert snow on the burning alkali flat. But that scene at Salt Fork in the shadow of the sand hills of nearly fifty years ago is still alive and moving in front of my eyes, and I can't wipe it away.

I can see the small red depot and the round gib-
bet of the railroad water-tower rimmed with the
stubs of old posse ropes. Somewhere along the Rio
Grande I can hear the whistle of the eastbound
train that was to take Lutie Brewton forever away
with the voices of lambs from the shipping pens in
her ears, almost human voices that might have been
those of little Jimmy and Brock and Sarah Beth
calling to her over nearly fifty miles of plain. And
I can feel the long-controlled but now violently
overflowing passion of my uncle standing there
with his gun belt buckled under his long-tailed,
gray broadcloth coat, while the man Lutie Brewton
had refused to name, but whom we all knew, was
coming toward us only a few hundred yards away,
somewhere just behind that cloud of emigrant
canvas.

I noticed that men were standing on the flat roof
of the Baca hide and wool warehouse and that the
teamster had finished loading his flat delivery
wagon with a high pyramid of flour, but made no
effort to drive it away. Above the bullet-punctured
fence around the Kingman Mercantile Company
store I could see a row of heads belonging to com-
mission-house clerks all turned toward the square.
And presently I became aware that young Lawyer
Archie Meade had left the side of the troubled

Henry McCurtin as if he couldn't bear to see what might happen to his approaching friend.

The train was whistling now by the small river ranchos and finally through the cottonwood bosque where of a summer afternoon the town boys played Jesse James. Some of the silent crowd, I saw, tried not to look up the street, but it was plain that everyone was standing there in a kind of strained expectancy, waiting for Chamberlain's creamy Western hat and brown-checked Eastern suit to appear.

Only Lutie Brewton refused to be still, throwing herself into saying good-by to her friends with an animated gayety that was almost incoherence, laughing to this one and chattering to that, hugging Myra Netherwood and dabbing quick kisses on Cora Holderness's cheeks, while her hands fluttered and flew and drew back like a pair of white falcons on the leash.

Some of the ladies were crying, although when Lutie Brewton turned to say good-by to me, I stood deaf and stony to hide everything I felt.

"Thank you for bringing my trunk," she said brightly, but when I was kissed, with the scent of violets swimming about me, she whispered in my long hair: " Say nice things about me to my babies till I send for them, Hal! "

And now without a sign as yet of Brice Chamberlain, the train was in, with black smoke drifting from the bulging smoke-stack, and with women passengers staring curiously at Lutie Brewton as their full skirts rustled to the train. My uncle himself carried her valises into the palace car, where I could see him standing by her seat as she gracefully chatted and laughed at her open window to her friends outside on the raised plank platform, her modulated voice clear and charming as if nothing had happened or could happen and she might be only taking a flying trip to Santa Fe.

Even after the conductor, who had waited respectfully for my uncle to alight, gave the signal for the train to start, and when she and everybody else knew that the man who was to be United States district attorney in Colorado had not appeared from that tangle of emigrant canvas to join her, Lutie Brewton sat there alone and gallant as I had ever seen her, leaning from the window to wave gayly and throw kisses to us all.

"Good-by! Good-by!" For a moment the air was filled with eager cries. Then she was gone. And suddenly the platform was silent and most curiously empty, and everyone stood there looking after the train that was already just a retreating door with a narrow window on either side and a streak of dark smoke drifting above it.

Only my uncle refused to look at it. With his head up and his dark eyes a warning to all he met, he walked toward the hotel, a lone, powerful figure to whom no one at the moment dared to speak.

vii

As soon as he was gone, the crowd stirred and moved about like a pack of small dogs that had been cowed by the presence of a mastiff. Several men I knew edged to the side of my uncle's lawyer.

" They say Brice Chamberlain's up with Archie Meade in his office now, Mr. McCurtin," one of them said. " What do you reckon Chamberlain'll do now — take the train tomorrow? "

Henry McCurtin's eyes were pits of gray granite in the mountainous bulk of his cheeks.

"Whatever Brice Chamberlain intends to do, he
certainly would not inform us, gentlemen." He
bowed, and moved stolidly up the street.

And so did I, as well as I was able, knowing no
more than Henry McCurtin. Contrary to my ex-
pectations, we stayed in town all next day and my
uncle drew a thousand dollars in cash from John
Kingman, who did a general banking business in
his store. And when the time came for the next
eastbound train, my uncle was on the plank platform again, with a tensely eager collection of human beings scattered for two hundred yards about
the depot, trying to be casual and inconspicuous,
clustered about wagons and leaning on saddle
horses and board fences tacked with signs of sheep
dip, liniment, and tobacco. One and all, friends or
enemies, my uncle ignored them, pacing implacably
up and down, a bulge still under one of the tails of
his coat, his great head thrown up like the breech
of a twenty-pounder, his pitch-black eyes from
time to time throwing a fearless look up the street.

Henry McCurtin told me afterwards he believed
my uncle had merely planned to take the train with
Brice Chamberlain and stay with him until he made
sure of his man. But Chamberlain did not appear

that day or the next. No one saw either him or his
gripsacks pass on the street, yet common knowl-
edge had it he was staying with his kin, the John
Holdernesses, from whose house a veritable stream
of telegrams, it was said, had begun to pour to
Washington.

For Lutie Brewton's sake I felt a kind of shame
for him, holing up like a fox or coyote here in Salt
Fork where everybody knew it. Even Archie Meade
seemed embarrassed by his part in the affair, crossing the square as if in a hurry to shut himself out
of sight in Brice Chamberlain's old office across the
alley from the Courthouse Saloon. And my uncle
bore a look of perpetual contempt on his rude face.

The fourth day he disdained to go to the depot,
and several evenings later he broke his silence to
me as we sat at supper in the hotel eating-room
under the mounted heads of antelope and the long
twisted horns of steers that supported rifles belonging to the diners.

" You can drive your buckboard back to the
ranch in the morning, Hal," he said, I thought, a
little wearily.

All week I had slept on the red sofa in the cavernous Bridal Chamber, still my uncle's room when he
came to town. I remember that when I went to bed
that night it was still dusk and so warm I threw the

covers over the pointed back of the sofa, carved with scrolls and curlicues. And when I awoke I thought a bunch of cowhands from some remote ranch had arrived in town for a rowdy night at the dance halls.

Then I was conscious of an unaccustomed light in the darkened room and, slipping over to the long window, I saw a procession from the emigrant camps winding around the plaza, all men, some on horseback, some on foot, in patched hickory shirts and linsey-woolsey shirts and faded blue and striped and gray denim jumpers.

A few carried long cap and ball rifles, but most of them held up hoes and pitchforks and American flags and two or three crude flares that threw waves of sultry light over their unshaven faces, the faces of tenant farmers from Kansas, of hunters from Arkansas, of Missouri backwoodsmen and Louisiana steamboaters and cotton choppers from East Texas and artisans and tradesmen whose living had been unsatisfactory in half a dozen Mississippi and Ohio River states.

I watched them pass, then pulled on my boots and clothes and ran down under the swinging red oil lamp on the hotel stairs. When I reached the street, it was empty, but I could see the nesters massed in front of the Holderness house, that stood

with proud head and shoulders above all the squat
adobe buildings of Salt Fork, the leaping flares
lighting up the impressively mortared bricks, the
yellow woodwork and round-eyed cupola on the
roof.

As I stood in the shadows of the livery stable,
a hoarse roar of enthusiasm rose from the emigrants, and I saw the familiar tall figure of Brice
Chamberlain on the Holderness front porch, showing himself at last. A bit pale even at this distance
in the flares, but resolved and still masterful in a
long coat, his blond hair brushed vigorously back
from his forehead, he advanced to the ornately
runged railing.

What he said at first I do not know, for he spoke
in a low tone. Then his voice rang down the street,
and I think it could have been heard in the square.

" This much I dare tell you," he challenged, and
I imagined I could see the blue fire in his eyes,
" that the President is my friend. And he won't
stand by in Washington while ruthless forces in
this backward territory oppose and oppress you.
That I can promise you as surely as I can that the
President of the United States today appointed me
judge of your district court. And I have no fear
but that he will see to it that the Senate confirms
my appointment."

A thunder of approval with shouts of "Judge Chamberlain!" swelled and echoed in the dusty street. But I scarcely heard it, standing there stiff and incredulous, aware that something unexpected and tragic had happened, something that Lutie Brewton with all her quick mind, that saw into everything like a slender golden sword, had not foreseen.

And neither had I until now when everything stepped into its proper place like Dagget's livery horses into their own stalls. And I could see that Brice Chamberlain, lawyer that he was, had moved to clear himself from my uncle's silent threat against the unnamed man going away with Lutie Brewton, and by the same stroke was vindicating himself in the eyes of certain Salt Fork people who would say now that the new judge had never intended to take the train to Denver at all.

All the way back to the hotel, I felt my anger rising against Chamberlain and wondered what Lutie Brewton would do now. And when I entered the room I was uncomfortable to find my uncle there, his shirt already off, the black growth curling on his chest like hair from a buggy cushion. He paid me no attention until he had worked off his boots and made himself ready for bed. Then he pinned me to the floor with his eyes that still mirrored a reflection of the emigrants' wild flares, and lifted a long leather wallet from the inside pocket of his removed gray coat with tails.

"Put this under your pillow," he said. "You're going to Denver tomorrow. I want you to find Lutie and give it to her. She'll need it."

"Yes, sir," I stammered, aware now that he knew of Chamberlain's change of appointment and thinking I would give almost anything rather than find Lutie Brewton in her humiliation. And yet somewhere in my blood I felt an inexpressible eagerness that I was to see her again.

I wanted to tell him what Brice Chamberlain had promised the nesters, but I didn't dare. Towering there in his long white night-shirt, his untamed black eyes and fierce dark hair and mustache, he reminded me of one of the uncontrollable Bedouin chiefs of whom I had read at school. Then he laid himself down on the huge Bridal Chamber bed, and even after I had undressed and blown out the light I could feel him there, powerful and motionless on his back, his eyes open, staring at the ceiling.

But some time during the night I heard him tossing and muttering. And once his voice came out thick and strong, like one of his roundup orders bawled above the din of cattle and men, although

what he said tonight was sinister and utterly in-
comprehensible.

"Drink your saddle galls, nesters!" it sounded
like. "You've got to plow deeper than that to find
him."

viii

THE BRILLIANT sunshine lay like a golden shawl
over the rich mountain city that morning my train
set me down for the first time in my life in young
Denver. The names of strange railroads incited me
from the sides of locomotives at the depot. As I
passed up Seventeenth Street, a babel of voices
from the doors of clothing stores, auction houses,
and pawnbroker shops coaxed and flattered me

68

with " sir " and " young gentleman." There was
something in the streets I walked that morning, in
the costly dress of the ladies in passing carriages,
in the very air that swept down from the mountains, something lavish, dashing and sparkling like
Lutie Brewton herself, and I thought I began to
understand a little of her fever for this prodigal
place that was growing by leaps and bounds.

Even in the business house of my uncle's friend,
George Twitchell, the lavish touch was there. I felt
I was walking on a silver floor as you did in the Silver Dollar Saloon, although the Twitchell establish-
ment was only a hardware house, the largest west
of St. Louis, with men from half a dozen states and
territories joking and telling stories as they bought
everything from six-shooters to mining machinery.
And when George Twitchell took me home to noonday dinner in a fabulous brick mansion behind a
tall ornamental fence where a wild Canada goose
with one clipped wing swam endlessly around in
a fountain, I knew that my uncle, who had said
nothing of Lutie Brewton coming back, was aware
that a thousand dollars would not let her stay in
Denver forever.

That afternoon with the wallet in my pocket,
with my hair freshly cut by a Denver barber, my
boots shined, and an impressive card supplied and

inscribed: " Mr. Harry Brewton " in George
Twitchell's blue Spencerian flourishes, I stiffened
my young back and pushed myself toward the new
Brown Palace Hotel.

A lively bevy of ladies rustled out as I came in.
They were hatted and gloved, in silks and satins,
with bows and puffs, and laces and flounces, chatting gayly to each other like a group of brilliantly
plumaged birds at one of my uncle's ponds on the
Cross B. They left the scent of violets and other
flowers floating behind them, and if I had doubted
it before, I was sure I should find Lutie Brewton
here now.

An elegant clerk with a small, trimmed beard, a
long tailed coat and immaculate stand-up collar
took my card in his fingers.

" Mrs. Colonel Brewton? " he repeated. " Oh,
yes, Mrs. Lutie Cameron Brewton." His face
lighted and at once he was treating me with respect.
I knew now that he had surely seen her and talked
to her, and for the moment it was almost as if she
were already there in front of me, stepping lightly
down the red-carpeted stairs, a lady no one need be
ashamed of here, crying: " Hal! " in her clear,
modulated voice and throwing her sensitive arms
about me.

Then I became aware that his face had clouded

and he was speaking to me with genuine regret.

" We all wished Mrs. Brewton might have stayed with us longer."

I stood there stiffly, aware that something beautiful was slipping out of my grasp. The clerk's hands, white as a lady's, were turning the leaves of a leather-bound ledger.

" Mrs. Brewton was here until day before yesterday," he said. " I think she received a letter or telegram. I remember she was very gay, but I had the distinct impression she had been disturbed. She paid her bill and left the hotel and gave us no address. I am very sorry."

When I stepped out into the street, the sun had vanished behind a cloud and the golden air of the city had fled. And all week while I called at the other hotels and boarding-houses, and while I watched from the mule cars for a delicate face and slender figure, and hung for whole afternoons along Broadway scanning the smart procession of ladies in carriages and fancy carts and rubber-tired runabouts, I never saw it again, although George Twitchell took me by night to the better restaurants, to the Tabor Grand Theater, and to a quiet brick house that upstairs turned into a great room of which I remember Soapy Smith in his black ministerial garb and ladies and gentle-

men gambling at a score of tables, scarcely notic-
ing huge paintings on the wall that made me blush
to my ears.

And when the week was done, all I had for my
pains was an endless picture gallery of faces that
kept passing me in my sleep, peering and staring
at me, ladies' faces, homely and beautiful, soft and
hard, sad and glittering. But none of them had that
rare something that was Lutie Brewton.

Monday morning I took my uncle's wallet from
one of the tall iron safes in the hardware house.

" She's probably gone home," George Twitchell
cheered me. " Where else could she go? You'll find
her sitting on the ranch-house porch when you ride
up."

He was a hearty man, tall and raw-boned, with
an air that begat confidence. But when I reached
Salt Fork and saw the old town with its dusty
streets and plank sidewalks asleep in the yellow
sun, I knew they had not been trod the last few days
by the slender, alive foot of Lutie Brewton.

On the sugary counter of his mercantile company John Kingman counted the money, his lips
moving through his heavy beard in time with his
fingers. Once his eyes strayed to the store porch
behind me. And when I had passed through the
wide-open front doors of the Dagget livery stable,

Frank Dagget's did the same. Then I understood.

"Hullo, Hal," he greeted. "See the elephant and hear the owl hoot up in Denver?" And when I nodded briefly, "Shorty Bowen took your buckboard. He said you could hire a buggy if you needed one."

"I don't need any," I said stiffly, knowing what he meant.

The liveryman looked indefinably disappointed.

"Shorty had to pack a couple cases of cartridges out to the ranch," he mentioned.

I felt my ears sharpen, but Frank Dagget's face held no more expression than one of his buggy curtains, neither then nor when he cinched up a horse for me while I forced open its mouth for the bit, a hard unwilling mouth that still dripped with the yellowish green of livery oats.

As I rode out the straggling street Lutie Brewton had walked with me that day now so long ago, Brice Chamberlain drove by me in a hired buggy and an impressive black frock coat like Judge White used to wear. He had always gone out of his way to cultivate my friendship, but today he greeted me with cool and scant ceremony, while I scowled at him in turn and wondered where he had been out here in a direction that led almost nowhere except to the remote ranches.

Then as my pony reached the top of the sand hills, I saw it, a cloud of emigrant canvas rolling where the escarpment fell away to the river, one united tent and covered-wagon city with horses and mules, oxen and milk cows grazing for miles on the mesa.

As the trail took me gradually closer, I grew aware of the unmistakable activity and excitement in the encampment; the sound of hammers on camp anvils and wagon wheels; the movement of nesters in and out of the canvas like ants; the men and women repacking scores of wagons, and voices calling exultantly to each other, while out on the mesa men and boys on horseback were herding the animals toward camp.

It was clear to me now where Brice Chamberlain had been. And if I hadn't guessed it then, I would have known it when I reached the ranch house that evening and found the bunkhouse almost an arsenal of six-shooters and Winchesters while out on the ground around the supper fire sprawled more Cross B hands than I had ever seen together at one time, tin plates of steak and biscuits in their laps, tin cups of black coffee in their hands, and a look in their eyes I well knew.

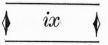

ix

I was glad for all the dark war clouds as an excuse
to put off reporting to my uncle about Lutie. But
in the end I knew that all the time he stood there in
the dim hall listening to what I had to say about
the nesters and questioning me about their camp
and numbers, there was only one person who walked
in his mind.

"You didn't see her?" he demanded at last.

I stammered what had happened in Denver. He made no comment. But when Black Hetty came in from the children's room to light a lamp, I saw that his great arrogant face was lined and his eyes held orange flames that I know now were hatred for the man who had failed Lutie Brewton. And the following day when one of our riders brought word that the nesters had left their camp near the river and already, as if it were a fiesta, were swarming in wagons and on horseback over the eastern part of our fertile big prairie, the violence poured into his face like a living flood that would tear out any dam in the country, and from the dark clouds of his eyes I could see that torrents of anger were still falling.

" Is Judge Chamberlain with the nesters? " he growled deep in his throat.

" I think it was him in a livery buggy," the cowhand stammered.

"Go out and tell the boys to saddle up," my uncle ordered.

I knew what that meant. And when the hand had gone, my uncle must have seen it in my face, for he fixed his fearful gaze on me.

" Remember, boy," he said, " there are times in your life you've got to be hard. No man respects

you for being soft to him today and letting him
ruin you and himself tomorrow. You're going to see
things before sundown that aren't nice to look at
and you better not come along if a college educa-
tion's made a woman out of you."

"I can be plenty hard to a nester," I told him.

Adamant in his gray broadcloth coat with its
tightly fitting shoulders and tails long spread by
the saddle; his long, wrinkled boots, far different
from the showy footgear of the modern West and
unblacked since Lutie Brewton had gone away, he
started for the corrals and the big buckskin I knew
he would ride today.

Then as we passed through the green wall of
cottonwoods and misty spraying tamarisks that
Lutie Brewton had had planted, I saw the hands at
the corrals and bunkhouse watching three horse-
men riding over the rise, the sun sparkling like
quicksilver on them and their saddle rigging. And
when they rode closer, I could make out blue uni-
forms and polished saber hilts, slouch hats with
gold insignia, and the straight-laced backs of officers from Fort Ewing.

My uncle had thrown up his head with that
lordly challenge of a wild stallion, and now he
waited there in a kind of rude and insolent magnifi-

cence until the rider of the bald-faced horse in the lead turned into Major Wilberforce, a soldier of dignity and fierce red mustaches.

He drew off a gauntlet glove and reached down from the saddle to shake hands.

" We're camping by the spring on your big vega, Colonel," he greeted. " We've got a troop of sixty-five men, and the Captain and I couldn't resist riding over to have dinner with you."

What he said was perfectly smooth and friendly, but I could see that our hands had stiffened and were watching my uncle, who stood there now with utter dignity, although his mustache seemed to bristle and his eyes were pitchforks. After what seemed to me an extremely long time, he inclined his head.

" Won't you gentlemen come in? Have your orderly feed your horses." With powerfully controlled steps and speech, he led the way back to the gallery of the ranch house.

All afternoon I watched the Major and the Captain perspire in their efforts to bring back the friendship of old times as they sat there facing their waiting host, drinking whisky on the tufted horsehair parlor chairs, telling stories of the service, with the children thumping and shouting at play somewhere in the big house, and dinner and supper in the familiar dining-room. No one mentioned Lutie Brewton's name, and yet it was plainly a mockery with her away and the nesters swarming like sheep over our big vega.

At the sound of their horses led to the gallery that evening, the officers rose with relief to ride back to camp. My uncle stood up.

" May I inquire, Major, who ordered the troops to my big prairie? "

The officer looked grave under his red mustaches.

" By order of the President, Colonel," he said in a low voice.

" The President," my uncle went on with pitiless irony, " wants you and your troops to stay for some time? "

"Until further orders, Colonel." The Major cleared his throat and looked up. " I hope we shall still be friends."

My uncle did not reply. He stood there with lips tight and eyes pitch-black with contempt for the man who had pulled strings for others to fight his battles for him. I could feel the bitterness working in him like the hot desert winds sweeping the cedars of the rocky canyons of Ladron. In the end the blue veins in his neck and hands gradually relaxed, and I knew the fury of the storm had for the time abated, that he would never send his men to fight against his country's troops, but would relentlessly put himself through the humiliation of sending them back to their respective camps in the morning.

" Good night, gentlemen," he said harshly when they left. " You can keep the nesters from being blown away, but God Himself can't the prairie! "

Long after they had gone, I watched him in the bright June moonlight that was almost like day, standing motionless on the gallery facing the big vega. And that night as I lay in my sleepless bunk staring into the white haze that entered my deep window, I fancied that in the milky mist I could see the prairie as I had seen it all my life and would never see it again, with the grass in summer sweeping my stirruped thighs and prairie chicken scuttling ahead of my pony; with the ponds in fall black and noisy with waterfowl, and my uncle's seventy thousand head of cattle rolling in fat; with the tracks of endless game in the winter snow and thousands of tons of wild hay cured and stored on the stem; and when the sloughs of the home range greened up in the spring, with the scent of warming wet earth and swag after swag catching the emerald fire, with horses shedding and snorting and grunting as they rolled, and everywhere the friendly indescribable solitude of that lost sea of grass.

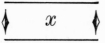

_x_

IT struck me as strange to see the sun come up as usual over the eastern plain next morning. And at breakfast I asked my uncle if I could ride west with the Red Lake hands to look for my missing B B mare. He raked me with his coal-black eyes, and I think he knew why I didn't want to stay, but he said nothing, and by the time we reached our Red Lake camp the summer rains were sweeping down from La Ceja.

All night the water dripped from the camp-house roof with a steady clop until my ears seemed to fill with the sound, and suddenly I knew that I hadn't got away from it at all, and what I heard in my brain was the clop, clop, clop of the cloven hoofs of oxen, of wheels slopping in the sloughs, of the gutturals of men and shrill voices of women, of crying babies and crates of cackling barnyard fowl, of the baas of sheep and goats and all the rest of the despised chattels of nesters scattering like a victorious army over our range.

When at last I rode reluctantly back to head-quarters, I could see them squatting in likely places on our big vega, digging holes for their dugouts like prairie dogs in the ground, or plastering with mud a frame of cedar poles from Ladron, stringing barbed wire where our cattle and horses and the antelope had always grazed free, or yelling at their teams of mules and steers as they tore up the virgin sod with a breaking plow.

Hot and almost trembling with anger, I came through the wide hall of the ranch house at late dusk and halted, a little ashamed of myself in the sitting-room doorway. Still the same rude, uncon-querable figure, my uncle sat with his great proud face over his tan leather account books as if there wasn't a nester within fifty miles, although I knew that from the near-by window he could have seen through the cottonwoods a half-dozen lights beginning to quiver across the dark prairie.

Sitting there that evening and other evenings between the heavy walls of the old ranch house, with my uncle's steel pen scratching arrogantly or his two-weeks-old Kansas paper rattling in lusty gusts in his hands, with my young cousins stretched on the floor cutting out paper horses and cattle from old magazines, and all around us the familiar curtains, furniture, and carpet by lamplight, the feeling kept creeping over me that Lutie Brewton was somehow still here. And once when a faint scent of violets seemed to rise in the room from one of her despoiled magazines, I could almost swear that her slender figure was there in the shadows behind me, alive, delicate, and sparkling, waiting before calling out in that high clear fun-loving voice she always used to children.

A few days later Black Hetty whispered to me portentously:

"Heah dem wagons a-rollin' by, Mistah Hal? Miz Brewton come back mighty soon now. It ain't lonesome round heah no mo'. No, sah. You wait and see if Hetty doan know."

It was true, I told myself half bitterly, that we weren't a peacefully remote ranch house any more,

forty or fifty miles from the nearest neighbor. From
the bunkhouse doorway you could see fences and
plowed furrows, and smoke rising from mud chim-
neys. Nearly every day nesters in spring wagons
or road wagons rattled by to town or to visit other
nesters. And nester children began to ride up on
the backs of old horses to borrow matches or sour-
dough leaven for biscuits or baking soda for a cow
with the colic.

They avoided the ranch house as they would a
pestilence, going straight to the bunkhouse. I saw
little Jimmy and Sarah Beth stand stiffly under the
cottonwoods watching them, but the tow-haired
Brock ran right up and tried to get them to stay
and play. It made me think of the time Lutie Brewton had run and shouted with the emigrant children, although these nester youngsters today were
like another race, mute, staring, defiant, and yet
scared. As soon as they climbed back on their
horse from a wagon wheel, they rode hurriedly
away. But I knew that Lutie Brewton would have
coaxed them to stay and talk and smile with a
glass of lemonade and a piece of democrat cake.

Once they were there as my uncle happened to
come riding in, and they huddled together as if they
had seen an ogre who would forbid what Will Lub-
bock, the bunkhouse cook, had just given them.

But if my uncle saw them, there was no sign of it. In his eyes lately when he came riding up to the ranch house was a look as if he faintly expected someone. Tomorrow, always tomorrow, I told myself, we would glance up and there she would be in one of Frank Dagget's livery buggies as if she had just been to town. Dagget himself would be looking pleased and proud for the Colonel. My uncle's face would be grave, and he would inquire with unfailing courtesy of her health and not a word about where she had been or the skunk who had failed her. And every day the headquarters hands would listen to her high clear voice when she called the children.

But July passed and August passed, and the night before I went back east to college, my uncle called me into the big front bedroom. I hoped that he would order me to see the nun, Mercedes, at the convent in St. Louis to ask if she knew where Lutie Brewton was. But he did not mention Lutie's name. Once he glanced at her glove still lying untouched like a delicate part of her, feminine, sensitive, and crushed, on a shelf. And deep in his eyes I saw red coals like the implacable Indian pueblo fires that are never allowed to go out. And the rest of the evening I could feel him far back in his mind stirring the charred embers and laying fresh logs on the blaze.

And when I lay down that night in my bunk I knew my uncle's inner convictions that wherever she was, the sensitive white hand of Lutie Brewton felt humiliated, dishonored, and crushed like its glove on the shelf, and that she would never come back and show herself to the ranch house and town that had idolized her — not even for her children.

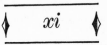

xi

For three long years, part of them in medical school, I didn't see the massive ranch house, not a grain of sand or blade of grass from the Cross B. I remember the weather as unseasonably dry those years at St. Louis, with the Mississippi gaunt as a trail-driven steer. But the Salt Fork weekly told in glowing italics of the heavy snows that fell west of Kansas and the unusual spring rains that soaked the ranges of the territory until they spouted like

the rock of Moses with springs. And every issue
there began to be more news of the nesters — emigrants, settlers, homesteaders, and agriculturists,
it called them — and less of the cattlemen, until a
thousand miles away my thumbs would bite through
the paper in anger.

More settlers were landing in Salt Fork by steam
and wagon train. The settlers were crowding the
Las Cruces land office. The settlers were plowing
up the rich brown prairie loam. The settlers were
harrowing and planting corn. From the sand hills
above Salt Fork the townspeople could see the vel-
vety green patches of the settlers' winter wheat and
rye. Judge Chamberlain said as the rains continued
that God was clearly on the side of the settlers. The
settlers' wheat stood golden in the sun. The heavy
heads of the settlers' rye knocked off men's hats.
And the settlers' corn could swallow up a horse and
rider.

Not that anyone would have known the existence
of a settler on the Cross B range from my uncle's
letters. Brief as always, the handwriting was still
spirited, erect and unquenchable as I had ever seen
it, with the final letter of every word sweeping up
like a lusty whiplash, and every proper name un-
derlined, not for emphasis, but from an overflow of
will and power.

But all those months he wrote me firmly that grass was good and beef high, that my B B mare had a pinto colt, that the hands and children sent me their best and he remained my uncle, Jas. B., I knew from other sources that his favorite saddle horse, Pompey, had thrown and tangled himself in nester barbed wire until he had to be shot; that in sheltered cañadas his cowhands were digging up the telltale buried horns and Cross B hides of butchered beeves; and that a score of nesters were suing him in Judge Chamberlain's court for the destruction by his cattle of their crops and gardens.

I expected the trial to be over before I came home. But in July when I stepped from the train, Salt Fork was like a nesters' holiday with grain wagons choking the square, and the sidewalks crowded with men often thick through the body as their gunnysacks of freshly thrashed wheat and rye, and most of them distinct from cowmen as a draft horse from a saddle pony. And everywhere in the stores the merchants were truckling to the nester women with the smiles and jokes I had thought they reserved for their cattlemen friends.

Standing on the steps of the old Exchange House, I could scarcely believe that this was the square for which only a few years ago I would grow desperately homesick. And when I looked for my

uncle in Judge Chamberlain's new brick courthouse where Clancy's dance hall used to stand, it
did not seem like the Salt Fork county court at all,
with no buckled spurs swinging on the railing, with
a floor of sawed pine, with pews for seats and all
these stolid spectators standing up as in church
while the tall figure of Brice Chamberlain swept
up to the bar with his bright blond hair waving
against the impressive black of his gown. Even the
Henry McCurtin I knew had vanished. With sagging cheeks and sunken eyes, he defended my uncle's case like a man who had had his first stroke of
paralysis and was calmly resigned to the second.

But it was when my uncle came in and the only
notice these sluggish-faced men showed for that
proud figure as he towered down the aisle were a
few sullen looks and a derisive muttering among
themselves that I felt the end had nearly come.

I tried not to listen to the court routine that followed, except when Judge Chamberlain, as if he
were rebuking a Mexican cow-thief, reviewed the
nester evidence against my uncle to the nester
jurors and charged them, as it sounded to me, that
they must find my uncle liable and fix the damages.
I was remembering a day twelve or fourteen years
before when only the whisper that the owner of the
Cross B was at the courthouse door had been

enough to stir the crowd's emotion. And when he had moved majestically down the aisle and through the railing with as much right as Judge White himself, the whole courtroom had been charged with his presence. And I realized that those golden wild horses of other days had slipped more deftly out of my uncle's rope than he knew, and would never be caught again.

First to go had been Lutie Brewton, then the sea of grass. And now these people who had waited till the West was safe and the pioneering done, were barking and snapping around my uncle's legs like a pack of dogs. They had him fairly surrounded, were raising their paws on him here and tearing out a piece of him there. But after I had watched him seat himself again in the old, fearless, unconquerable way, without so much as a glance at the nesters beside him, I knew that although he had lost his case they didn't have him down.

From where I sat I could see only the back of his head like some dark, shaggy Jove. And yet I was sure that the red coals of his eyes had fastened themselves on Brice Chamberlain, who might not realize it, but still had a debt to pay. Times might have changed, but my uncle never would change, never would forget till he died.

I remember that when I stepped out on the

street I found that the two boys had come along
to town with their father. When Brock saw me, he
pulled off Jimmy's hat, waved it, ran up the plank
sidewalk until he was about to be caught, and
sailed the hat toward a nester wagon loaded with
towsacks of wheat. For a moment the hat hung
against the sky. Then it missed the wagon and
fell into the deep mud.

Little did I think this night that the placid blue
sky I saw was already returning to its old mysterious cycle, that this was the last deep mud and one
of the last wagonloads of wheat that would be seen
in Salt Fork for what the Navajos north of Red
Lake called a land of snows.

xii

AT the time I thought it only the way the cards happened to fall. But when I look back on it now, it seems immutable and fixed as a chapter out of Genesis or Exodus, with the nesters safe on their Promised Land; with my uncle pushed back with his cattle on a thousand hills; with Brice Chamberlain in the seats of the mighty; and all the time the red eye of God watching from the burning bush,

not to see that what was to come would be humane
and sweet and according to progress, but that it
should be cruel and just and true according to the
book of destiny which blinds a man from properly
reading it until those who would dictate it are
dead and fifty or a thousand years have passed.

When the news reached me that the weather west
of Kansas and Indian Territory had changed, it
was as if the God few of us medical students believed in was in His heaven after all, and my eyes
must have burned with a deep exultation in the
dark halls of my school and hospital. The nester
women were praying for rain. The nester men were
hauling water from my uncle's ponds and wind-
mills. The more responsible nesters were packing
up to journey farther west and north, some to join
the Mormons. And Judge Chamberlain had made a
Fourth of July oration that it was the greatest
drouth in the history of the territory. But a letter
signed " Cattleman " to the paper said it was no
drouth at all, just normal old-fashioned New Mexican weather, and pointed to the native wild grasses
that had not been plowed under. With a desperate
skill born of long experience in this dry land, they
had caught the diminished rains and rushed into
growth and seed while the nesters' corn and wheat
scarcely sprouted in the ground.

On my way home through Missouri and eastern Kansas the following spring, a veil of gray mist hugged the car windows. But once the train had climbed the high plateaus, the windows were clear, the skies a dull blue, and the plains toasted brown with sod. And when we came close to Salt Fork I had a glimpse from the train of puffs of dust moving over the prairie that were nesters plowing and harrowing a dry land.

I hadn't seen my uncle since I left, and I felt he would be almost insolent with triumph to be vindicated at last. Then I stepped off the train at the familiar red depot and he was there with his buggy to meet me himself, and I wasn't sure of his feelings at all. With his great face plowed and harrowed, his mustache turning gray, but his eyes still pitch-black as I had ever seen them, he drove me home over what had once been his fertile range and was now a waste of barbed wire and bare ground and squalid gates to open and close, with a few of the dugouts empty and already falling in, and the song of an occasional mocking bird or meadow lark a mockery in the dead and dying young fruit trees. And I can still see him sitting in his buggy, silent and deaf, while a nester in an unwashed undershirt tried to sell him his barren, proven-up fields.

It was long after dark when we reached home.

The earthen ranch house stood deep in the shadows of its cottonwoods and tamarisks like a forgotten fortress decaying in its ancient bosque. Sarah Beth was east at convent school, the boys asleep in bed, and I saw where, during my uncle's absence in town, the spring winds had deposited miniature dunes of sand and nester field dust along the wall boards as if no walls were there.

And that evening as we sat at the great hulking supper-table, bare of cloth and candles, with only the smoky light from a brass lamp trickling over us; and afterwards as I wandered through the rude hall and silent parlor with boys' quirts and ropes, spurs, bridles, and saddles scattered over the floor, and boys' rough fingerprints and boot-marks on the dusty lid of the piano; and again next morning when I heard the two boys fighting and tumbling like young savages over the parlor floor and then riding off hard on their ponies, it seemed strange to think that there had ever been a gentle lady in the house.

" She's gone and nobody but my uncle remembers her any more," I told myself, getting up from the bunk where she had once nursed me with the whitest and lightest of hands.

But when I rode out to the remote Cross B camps in the cedar-dotted hills where the nesters had not yet penetrated, and when I talked to some of her old friends in town, I found that they were still talking of the beautiful wife of Colonel Brewton.

Several thought they knew where she was. Young Mrs. Bob Kingman said she had seen Lutie Brewton's face, as young and beautiful as ever, in a nun's wimple on the streets of New Orleans. The gentlemanly wagon boss of the Bar 44, who had won a prize with her as his partner at whist, had seen someone he believed was Mrs. Brewton in a stunning black lace gown and diamonds gambling for high stakes in Tombstone. She was painted and powdered like a dance-hall woman, but he had absolutely remembered the feverish gestures with which she played. And John McCandless, agent for the Mescalero Apaches, had gone to Washington on Indian bureau business and seen a lady he knew but couldn't place, in an open carriage on Pennsylvania Avenue, by the side of a foreign ambassador or someone with ribbons on his coat. She had flushed when stared at and turned her head, and not until they were by did he realize it had been Mrs. Brewton.

Myra Netherwood thought Lutie must be dead. But the story I clung to was told by Superintendent Bedford of the railroad, who had been at the famous Silver Ball given with full orchestra and waxed floor under a waterproof canopy at the bottom of a Colorado silver mine. During the evening a fall of rock in a near-by stope had frightened the dancers off the floor, all but a guest with another name, who was the image of Mrs. Brewton. For several minutes while the rocks continued to fall, she had kept on gayly dancing with her partner, encouraging the orchestra and laughing to her partner as if nothing had happened, until most of the guests were over their scare and back on the floor. Somehow I felt that had been the real Lutie Brewton, and the peculiar emotion I had always felt at the sight of her had welled up in me indescribably at the story.

But later I found that there was something else they were saying about her, although they did not say it to me. And I was to learn that nothing was too romantic and fantastic to speculate about Lutie Brewton.

All I noticed at first was that they took a great interest in young Brock when he came with me to town, laughing at his quick replies and provoking him to others. And all the while the ladies admired his feathery blond hair and treated him to slices of layer cake, and while the men bribed him to strut up and down the Kingman store porch like certain well-known characters of town, I could see them exchange veiled glances and knowing nods. And yet for a medical student I was thick in the skull as a nester and thought nothing of it until in August when we had all driven to town to meet Sarah Beth, who was coming home alone by train from convent school in the morning.

The square swarmed as usual with nester wagons and all their nondescript conveyances, as if having a poor crop year meant nothing to them. My uncle's old friend Dr. Reid, as one professional man to another, invited me into the White Elephant Saloon, and I found several nesters drinking next year's wheat, appropriating the front of the long walnut bar. A little group of cattlemen and cowhands kept themselves distinct at the other end, and while I shook hands with several of them, the doctor gravely waited for me. His face and manner were courteous and serene, but I knew his hand was twitching to wrap itself around a dark bottle, a long white hand marked with veins that as a small boy I was sure must flow with purple wine.

The screen had been moved back from the open door, and across the street I could see young Brock and Jimmy facing each other on the Holderness porch steps as if they had had one of their usual differences and the men around them were tactfully stirring them up to fight. The two boys made a

picture I can see now against the rough splintery
background of the store, with colored tin signs
tacked on the step rises and against the red wall
— Jimmy, slim and dark, like a small, stiff image
of his father, fists tightly clenched — and Brock
leaning forward recklessly to hit him on the nose,
his hat pushed back where it hung by its throat
latch, his hair a kind of white gold in the afternoon
sun.

Then it happened. A bushy, round-headed nub-
bin of a nester in a hickory shirt ridged like cor-
duroy moved to the doorway.

"I'm a-bettin' on the Chamberlain young 'un,"
he called.

For a split fraction of a second as his meaning
broke over me, I saw Lutie Brewton clear and beautiful as I had ever seen her in the life. And when
the nester turned and grinned toward a sand-box,
it was almost as if he had spat in her face. I was
aware of the grave silence of the cowmen and of a
curious wild hate sweeping over me like prairie fire.
I had thought myself a medical student soon to go
out in the world and save human lives. Now I found
that the thin veneer of Eastern schools had cracked
and I was only a savage young Brewton from an
untamed sea of grass, moving through the little
gate where customers' rifles and pistols stood or

lay in their accustomed places on the back bar. I
was aware of the cowmen backing out of range and
of the bar-keeper ducking. And then I almost
wanted to kill Dr. Reid, too, one of whose white
hands had with surprising force suddenly thrown
up my barrel so that oil from a brass hanging lamp
started to pour on the walnut bar.

At the sound of the shot, men from the square
began to wedge their heads in the saloon doorway
until they were brushed aside like flies and my
uncle stood there, sniffing the smell of black powder
like an old war-horse, his black eyes sweeping the
room until they halted on me standing at the end
of the bar with my unsuccessful six-shooter in my
hand.

" What's going on, Hal? " he demanded.

I did not dare look at him now, only stood there
rigid with my lips closed tight. He waited what
seemed a half-hour.

"What was said in here, Walt? " he asked a
huge uncomfortable cattleman with open vest and
silver watch-chain tangled across it.

The sweat poured from the cattleman's forehead,
but he only shook his head. Something came into
my uncle's great face. For some little time more he
stood there unruly and aroused, dominating the
long dim room like old times. Then, following the

direction of a half-dozen glances, he turned his head and I saw that Jimmy and Brock had squirmed through the jammed doorway and were now standing there in the barroom with their black and white contrasting heads.

Just whom my uncle looked at the long minute he kept his head turned, I do not know, but I found it was Brock's eager young face and bright blue eyes I was staring at. In that short time I think there passed through my mind everything I had ever seen him do and heard him say, one minute mean and irrepressible, and the next charming and winning as Lutie Brewton herself so that you forgave everything. I remembered his taking to the nesters like his mother and how painstakingly impartial my uncle treated both boys, one like the other, always buying two when he bought one, and dividing equally the lash of his quirt although I felt that Brock usually deserved the most of it. And I wondered if this unnamable thing could have been the source of the deep-seated enmity between the two brothers ever since they had been old enough to walk, or what in God's name it was.

When my uncle finally turned, I saw that something unutterable and terrible had come into his face.

" If any dog has something more to say, now is

the time to say it!" he challenged them all, a wild violence fairly leaping from his dark eyes.

There was no sound in the long saloon but a chip someone dropped at a poker-table, the jingle of a horse shaking his harness at a hitching-rack, and the slow drip of oil on the bar like a clock ticking off the last minutes of the one who would speak. Then with almost a grimace of pain, my uncle nodded at me, and with the boys ahead of me, and my uncle to the rear, we pushed out into the square

PART III

Brock

xiii

It was the boy Brock I couldn't get off my mind the next few winters as a student assistant of a high-tempered French surgeon who operated at St. Mary's and the Alexian Brothers' hospitals. And I can't smell chloroform today without some of those old doubts and questionings rising up in front of me like ghosts. All the baffling memories I had of the boy kept turning over in my mind. Young

Brock playing he was a priest and singing mass in his high soprano to a herd of grazing longhorns. And young Brock playing posse with the nester children and hanging the outlaw, which was a stray dog, to a nester gate-post. Young Brock leading the half-starved nester youngsters over to the ranch house for sour-dough biscuits and vinegar pies. And young Brock sharpening the rowels of his spur with a blacksmith's file. Young Brock's white hands galloping gracefully through *Black Jack Davey* and *The Gypsy Maid* on the keys of Lutie Brewton's square piano. And the same white hands keeping a tomato-can rolling at fifty feet with the thirty-caliber, rim-fire five-shooter my uncle let him carry because it was hard to get the odd-sized cartridges.

It was Brock loving to talk. And Brock loving to ride. And Brock trading forty-five cartridges from his father's stores two to one for thirty rim-fire. It was Brock shrewd as a judge and reckless as a Brewton and charming and magnificent as his vanished mother as he swindled his and Jimmy's tutor out of their lessons for the afternoon. And all the time his feathery blond hair kept blowing this way and that in my mind.

Peaceably as if he had been a bishop going to his reward, old Dr. Reid back in Salt Fork made ready

to depart his life and his well-thumbed books of
Robert Ingersoll in his room at the Exchange
House, where the older guests would no longer hear
his bedside glass and whisky bottle striking the
hours of the night. And my uncle telegraphed for
me to come home and take the practice.

When I walked up the sandy boardwalk from
the train to the hotel, I found the old doctor in a
coma. I tried to make him as comfortable as I
could, but there was little I could do for him. Even
the bottle had been drained of its comfort, and he
knew neither me nor my uncle, who, when I came in,
had been sitting there for several hours quietly
smoking, as the two old friends had often sat in
health with only an occasional word between them.

" The thoughts of the señor doctor viejo are not
any more on this world," the Mexican woman who
had been taking care of him told me.

Once Brock burst eagerly into the room, star-
tling me as some blond Lutie Brewton in boots and
spurs, shaking my hand now like a grown man,
showing the gold piece he had won at monte, and
paying no attention to the bed and its burned-out
ember of a man who had brought him into the
world. But while the boy stood there laughing and
talking, fetching into the sick-room an air like a
fresh wind blowing from out of the past, I saw a

vestige of life and consciousness struggle into one of the old physician's eyes as if deep down in a well a man with a candle was trying to see and recognize the man at the windlass.

And after Brock had gone whistling down the hall, his boot-heels softened by the red carpet, his spurs jingling a purposefully manipulated tune, the old doctor tried slowly to sit up in bed.

" When did Mrs. Brewton come back? " he asked, staring at me, and I did not dare to look at my uncle, whose puffs on his cigar, I was aware, had suddenly ceased.

" I haven't seen her, doctor," I said in a low voice.

The light went out of his eye like the flame of a candle blown upon and he sank back, his long white hand with its veins of purple wine relaxing on the coverlet. But long after he was silent, the emotion I had always felt at a meeting with Lutie Brewton kept flooding and stirring me at the unexpected sound of her name.

We buried him a week or two later in one of those inexpressibly lonely and barren Southwestern graveyards, so different from the green graves he had known as a boy in his native Virginia. But the mourners, standing there with their hats off as men did forty years ago, did not see that. They were covertly watching the picture of Brock, taller than I, his blond feathery hair faintly yellow, standing only a few feet away from Judge Chamberlain, now a bit portly and distinguished-looking in a long black coat, a shiny high hat in his hand, his yellow hair faintly touched at the temples with silver, but still sweeping back over his head in a kind of masterful distinction.

And from then on, everything I remember of my uncle and Brock is tinctured with iodoform and carbolic acid of the old doctor's office that became my own, with its green student lamp shining on the white shelves of drug jars and bottles, on the old leather operating-couch strewn with surgical instruments, and on the skeleton that ever since I could remember had stood in a corner.

Before I was back in Salt Fork a year, I found that Brock was already becoming almost as well known a figure in Salt Fork as Ingram Carter, the gambler, whose full-length portrait in oil hung in the White Elephant Saloon. It was blond, gentlemanly Brock Brewton, a favorite with all the dark-haired dance-hall women in Madame Nana's Sala de Baile, and the same Brock Brewton never losing caste but sedately dealing whist and euchre from the best horsehair furniture in town. It was Brock Brewton playing the *Blue Danube* waltz

on Myra Netherwood's grand piano, and Brock
Brewton driving up and down the town streets with
his Choctaw-blooded nester girl beside him on the
seat of his red-wheeled open buggy.

And it was Brock Brewton buying out a show-
case of candy for the nester children standing
around like orphans in the Kingman Mercantile
Company store, and the same Brock Brewton
shooting Mrs. Olson's three white ducks almost out
of her hand while she fed them as he galloped by.

I can still see him in a long-legged brown suit
that reminded me of the one Brice Chamberlain
had once worn, taking his mother's friend Myra
Netherwood devoutly to mass. And I can see him
in the same suit, his hat pushed back recklessly
and his yellow hair curling, calling for a hundred
or two hundred dollars' worth of chips at the White
Elephant or Dutch Charley's.

He didn't pay for his chips like ordinary people.
He was a Brewton, and if he had called for a thousand dollars in gold, they would have tried to give
it to him, the bartender marking it down as usual
in his jaw-bone book. And when the Colonel came
to town, he would have asked for his bill and there
on the wet bar written out a check drawn on the
Kingman Mercantile Company.

Brock and all his conflicting ways, together with

my uncle's affection for and indulgence toward him, were one of the most puzzling things I had ever tried to solve. Perhaps it was that I refused to see Lutie Brewton as the others did, that to me she was still a young boy's beautiful lady. And it was summer with the bee balm in blossom again along the trail in the cañadas when fate tried to make me see it their way.

I had been called to a prairie dugout where a nester woman had tried to kill herself. She was very low and I couldn't leave her with her small baby fifty miles from a doctor. And several afternoons later when it was all over, I felt that I was no physician at all, only a tired and defeated ranch boy, and that I wanted nothing so much as to spend a night again among the old familiar things under my uncle's roof.

I was glad I had come. It was dusk when I approached the old ranch house and found light gleaming from a dozen windows, as I had often seen it in the past. And when I stepped into the bare old hall, I had the strange feeling that a lady was there. For a moment the incredible notion came to me that Lutie Brewton had returned. Then Sarah Beth in a girlish white dress with red sash and cuffs sprang out of the massive dining-room doorway and cried a welcome to me and said that she had

finished school forever and come through Salt Fork
the very morning I left.

They laid a place for me at the table. The white
dinner candles and their shades which I had not
seen since Lutie Brewton left, the great mass of
pink bee balm in the center of the huge old table,
and all around me the familiar heavy silver on
snowy damask affected me strongly. And all
through the meal I observed that my uncle sat very
quietly on his chair, the faint desert glow warming
his weather-beaten face as I had not seen it for
many a year, his pitch-black eyes softening a little
as they rested on Sarah Beth. But far back in his
eyes I had the impression that it was someone else
with dark hair and slender bare arms he saw sitting
here with other guests around a gayer and younger
table.

We were in the parlor, Sarah Beth had opened
the old piano and played some of her convent
pieces, and my uncle said he wished Brock were
home from town to hear them, when Jimmy was
called outside. With the room very still, Sarah
Beth's hands strayed into a waltz the name of which
I do not know but which her mother's white hands
had often played on the same black and yellow
keyboard when the room was filled with guests

from Fort Ewing to Santa Fe. I saw my uncle hold his cigar motionless in his hand, and for a minute or two with that old melody in the room it was almost as if the plague of nesters had never swarmed and that any minute Black Hetty might appear at the doorway with the three small children to give their mother good-night.

The feeling was so strong that I glanced up at the doorway, and found Jimmy standing there. I thought for the moment he was listening, then I was conscious of the tautening tendons in his tanned young face. And before Sarah Beth had finished, he moved rigidly to where his father sat quiet and proud on the big horsehair armchair.

" I just heard," he said in a low voice, " that Brock shot Dutch Charley in town."

Sarah Beth went on playing without hearing and my uncle, who still seemed to be in Lutie Brewton's waltz, sat staring at the boy as if the latter had told him that several Cross B cows were bogged down in Red Lake and his loose and bitter lower lip was considering whether or not to send hands at this hour to pull them out.

" Brock shot who? " he repeated, lowering his great head like a powerful bull trying to protect himself from a deep wound already administered.

Guessing that something was wrong, Sarah Beth stopped playing. Somewhere on the trail we could hear a galloping horse. Then Jimmy's low answer came clear enough in the huge room.

" Dutch Charley. He claimed that black-haired woman that deals monte for him was in with Brock and favoring him. He said every time Brock came to the table, the house lost money. They had an argument. Charley went for his gun, but Brock got him before he could shoot."

Sarah Beth gave a little cry, but my uncle had hold of himself now and was sitting up slowly with his old iron will and power. Only the faint gray showed through his deeply lined face.

" Is Charley dead? " he asked after a little.

" I don't know," Jimmy said. " They locked Brock up."

I knew that must have hit my uncle, but he was sitting there like some rude czar in gray broadcloth and linen, his great unruly face written with the ruthless, almost dissolute pride I remembered, and there was no change in it as Jimmy gave him, bit after bit, what the hands had told him. Only when the boy mentioned the name of Judge Chamberlain did my uncle show emotion, throwing up his head with the old untamed lustiness while his shaggy gray hair bristled.

" What did Chamberlain have to do with it? " he demanded.

By the whiteness of the boy's knuckles I knew that he guessed more than I had supposed. He tried to evade it, but his father's violent eyes were pinning him to the floor and he struggled against them uselessly.

" Judge Chamberlain is the one who got Brock out," he said in a barely audible tone. " He said it was because Brock was so young and he wanted to make a private investigation in the circumstances. If Brock behaves himself, he said the case might not come up at the next term of court. But Brock's got to report to Judge Chamberlain as often as he says."

For a headlong, incredible moment it was as if I had seen the long arm and white hand of Brice Chamberlain, like that of a groomed and masterful colossus, reaching across all Salt Fork county in front of the nesters and the livery-stable loafers, in front of the town ladies, the ranchers' wives and the dance-hall women, to pin a final ugly red brand on the gay, slender figure of Lutie Brewton.

I had seen my uncle angry many times, but never when his blood ran black in his veins as it did now. His face was like a dark storm from which the lightning was constantly hurling. Even across the

room I could feel, as physically as I can waves of
heat, the rising torrent of flame that, once aroused
in him, burned like a prairie conflagration that
no man could put out or stand up in front of, but
must be let to run its own wild and volcanic course.

Then I saw that he had risen to his feet and was
moving toward the door, and I don't think he knew
any longer that we were in the room, but all of us
knew where he was going. We watched him stop
and pick up his old sweated gun belt where it hung
from the post of a pine settee in the hall. And at the
sight of it, Sarah Beth rose quickly from her stool
and moved as far across the room as the painted
china parlor lamp on its tall ornamental brass and
marble stand.

"Don't go tonight, papa!" she begged him.
"Let Hal and Jimmy go in tomorrow."

He stood there bleak and unhearing, strapping
the double buckles of the belt before he turned and
swept the three of us with his violently smoldering
eyes that told us how far we could go and no farther, and that he was still lord of his family, in-
cluding Brock.

But he did not go. He stood there for a little in
the wide hall as if listening. Presently we heard
a familiar footstep on the gallery and Brock, his
yellow hair curling like a child's, came swinging

past him and into the room as fresh and gallant
and unscathed as I had ever seen him.

He must have guessed from all our faces that we
knew, and it only made him more charming and
desperately gayer, throwing himself into lively
banter at Sarah Beth as if she wasn't standing
there with white cheeks in front of him, ready to
burst into tears on his shoulder; chiding her for
not waking him up where he slept in the hotel most
of the day when she passed through town; laughing
and chattering and grimacing; teasing her about
Tom Milledeaux's love letters which the nuns rig-
orously read; and penitently coaxing her to play
a duet with him at the piano, where he pulled up
a horsehair chair and sat with one arm around her
waist while the other ran a brilliant accompaniment
on the lower part of the keyboard.

And I thought that no one in the territory, and
perhaps no one anywhere but Lutie Brewton herself, could have come in at a moment like this and
so disarmed us and held off my uncle until I saw
him take again his horsehair armchair, where he
sat waiting for the festivities to be over, the eyes in
his great intractable face watching Brock with
painful and unutterable affection.

At last Sarah Beth went to bed, and my uncle sat
looking at the boy.

"I was just starting to town to talk to you, Brock," he began. "Is it true you shot Dutch Charley?"

The boy's face intangibly changed, and he stood there watching my uncle through narrowed eyes.

"I had to shoot him or he'd have shot me."

"Is it true," the older man went on with dogged patience, "that the woman who deals monte for Dutch Charley was favoring you and you knew it?"

"All women like me," Brock said. "Like everybody liked — " His lips closed, but he kept his cool, veiled, almost derisive eyes on my uncle.

The slow color rose in the latter's rude leathery cheeks.

"I don't mind the shooting so much," he said with difficulty. "Boys will fight, and I wouldn't think much of you if you couldn't defend yourself. I told you I'd pay your gambling debts so long as you played fair and square. But I've always told you that cheating was the lowest form of animal life. Now you've cheated, and no matter what anybody else says, I want you to go through trial on your own feet until you clear yourself or take your punishment."

The boy was staring at him with a sudden curious, impersonal hatred.

" No father," he said defiantly, " would send his
boy to prison when the judge got him out of it.
Besides, I have a job. That's why I'm out here tonight. I'm going to be a counter jumper for
George Holderness and Company."

At the sound of the name of Brice Chamberlain's
uncle and all it implied, my uncle sat up and the
veins swelled in his throat and hands until even
the boy was afraid of him and backed across the
room. But his eyes were burning in his white face
with a restless and brilliant fever, and when he
saw he wasn't going to be touched, he began to
pace up and down the room.

" You can't keep me out on a ranch! " he was
crying. " I'm eighteen. I wasn't cut out for ranch-
ing. I've got to be where there's excitement and
people. I've got to be where there's stores and lights
and music and things going on. Sooner than stay
out here in this God-forsaken place, I'd rather be
stuffed in a coffin — "

I did not hear any more. There was something
fatalistic in the scene and words, as if I had been
here before. My uncle and Jimmy seemed to be gone
and I was on the same horsehair sofa seeing Lutie
Brewton pacing up and down this very Brussels
carpet, her eyes burning with a brilliant fever, her
lips speaking almost the identical words.

When I looked at my uncle, his face was white and he was breathing heavily as if he had seen a ghost.

"All right, Brock," he brought out thickly. How much it cost him, I could only guess. "I stood in the way of somebody else years ago and I've always been sorry. I won't stand in yours."

Flashing a look of triumph at the dark silent face of his brother standing there, Brock went quickly out of the room. Long after he had gone my uncle sat in his chair staring out of the window. The window was dark and he could see nothing outside, I knew, but I could see him in the pane and I never realized before how utterly furrowed his face was, like a worn-out field, the face of an old man at last. And the rest of him there on the tufted horsehair chair was the once powerful frame of a man in whom some inward drouth had dried up the last few water-holes of life and power.

Only his eyes were the same, burning black and unspeakably bitter in their charred sockets. After a while he rose unsteadily, paying no attention to Jimmy and me standing helplessly by. Then brushing aside Jimmy's proffered help and planting his boots slowly but relentlessly in front of him, he went on without speaking to his lonely and barren bedroom.

◆ *xiv* ◆

THERE was a huge cottonwood that used to stand off the plaza in one of Salt Fork's crooked Mexican streets. Its bark was rougher than any tree I knew and its branches gnarled. It had seen Navajo and Apache raids and the long ox trains crawling on the Chihuahua trail. But it still stood there green and cool, sheltering a lowly adobe house beneath it and all who passed under its branches or pulled chairs into its broad shade.

Of late the nesters had been tying their bony horses to it, and the horses had chewed off half its bark. The lightning had struck it, and the woman of the house and her young son had tried to cut it down. And when of a morning I crossed the plaza to my office, I found myself glancing to see if the old tree had weathered last night's storm.

Back in my mind, I think, it was really not the tree I looked to see if it were still standing there with its roots in the territory and its head in the sky, but an old man who wasn't there at all, who had also known the Navajo and Apache raids and the long ox trains crawling on the Chihuahua trail and now knew the winds that in my profession usually blow in the night.

One evening just before the fall term of court came around, Dutch Charley died of his gunshot wounds in his rooms over the saloon, and some time during the night, Brock left the dim lights of Salt Fork and an empty money-box of Holderness and Company behind him. I had not seen my uncle since the evening after the shooting. It had not been pleasant to think of him coming to town where everyone would see for himself how deeply he had been stricken. And now it was my conviction that he would not be in Salt Fork, if at all, for a long time to come.

But only a day or two later I met him walking across the plaza, slower, grayer, not much more than a shadow of his old powerful self, yet still painfully erect and implacable in his gray broadcloth tails as I had ever seen him. And the men looked sober when they saw him coming, and said with respect: " Gettin' dry, Colonel," and " Yessirree, Colonel," and looked after him thoughtfully when he had passed.

And when the news came that Brock had been seen in El Paso and called himself Brock Chamberlain now, everybody said it was all over and that you could take one look at Jim Brewton and know he himself admitted it. Certainly I seldom heard him mention Brock's name again. But it wasn't over. Once at Sarah Beth's wedding I thought I saw those burned-out eyes deep in their sockets keep staring dully at the guests as if there were someone missing in that familiar ranch-house parlor, although exactly who was missing I could never be quite sure.

I believe now that every piece of news about Brock my uncle read in the Albuquerque and Denver papers was a secret Apache lance in his heart. His forehead was incommunicable as an old rawhide and branded like one with the mark of the band of his hat. And of what went on behind it he

never spoke. All I know was that as months passed
and the stories kept coming in about Brock raking
eight thousand dollars from a Cripple Creek gambling table and Brock holding up a Mexican sheep
herder with three pesos on his person; of Brock a
deputy in White Oaks for a day and Brock that
night hitching a peddler's cart behind his saddle
and shooting up the town; of Brock riding south
into Old Mexico ahead of the sheriff, Brock riding
west with Cochran's Wild Bunch to hide in the
Chiricahuas and Brock riding east alone to bring
a jeweled necklace to his Choctaw-blooded nester
girl in our next county, he wasn't real to me any
more.

He was just a glittering idea, someone I had
never seen or known, only a name whose exploits
were printed in the Western papers from Omaha
to Oregon, talked about over wet bars and dry
trails, from horseback to horseback, in the harness-
rooms of livery stables and around lonely cow-
camp fires.

And when they came to me in my office to drive
forty miles into the next county to dress the
wounds of a deputy who could not be moved, I
sent word to Jimmy to keep it from my uncle, although it was all fantastic and unreal to me. This
Brock Chamberlain, wanted for a dozen things

over Arizona Territory, now making fools of a
county posse nearer home, holding off twenty or
thirty men from an abandoned nester's shack until
the sheriff had sent for Judge Chamberlain to come
and talk the boy into giving up, could not be the
Brock whose feathery white hair had blown with
my breath in his cradle.

Then suddenly I knew I was mistaken. The
morning train had come and gone, and I was refill-
ing the small bottles of my medicine valise and
picking up my surgical instruments when a step
sounded in the outer office, and when I looked up,
Lutie Brewton was standing there. Oh, her veil
hung heavy and dark and I could not distinguish
a feature beneath it, and she wore clothes I had
never seen before, but there was something in the
straining high angle of the plumes of her hat that
rang in my ears like calomel.

"Hal!" she said to me in the voice I hadn't
heard for fifteen years.

Even without eyes or ears I would have known
her. She hugged me in that silent integral part of
speech of several generations ago which told things
the lips neither would nor could. The familiar scent
of violets closed around me again like some delicate,
faintly purple cloud. And I was back in a world
ten thousand times larger than the brain that con-

tained it, still a long-haired ranch boy, Lutie
Brewton had never gone away, and my uncle still
rode the range in his lusty prime.

She pinned back her veil, not with the eager gesture of youth I remembered, but almost defen-
sively, and I saw that with all her struggled erect-
ness, her face, dead white against the lifted black
plumes, had begun to show the first branding marks
of her hated arch-enemy, age. As if she knew I had
seen, she threw herself into holding me at arm's
length, inspecting me with that critical yet flatter-
ing air, telling me almost feverishly how proud she
was of me as a doctor, that any woman just to see
me must throw herself in my care, and that as a
physician's ears must be filled with the woes of his
patients, she knew I should never ask her the weary
question where she had been all these years.

And I found myself gazing at that brilliant,
animated face and asking under my breath if it
were true that a few minutes ago I had seen any
signs of age. But all the time she plied me with
questions about Jimmy and Sarah Beth and Sarah
Beth's husband, whom she had never seen, I knew
it was Brock that had brought her. And it was
strange how I could feel him now for the first time
in years, one of those three sleepy youngsters
around her in their nightgowns in that early,

candle-lit room so long ago, peering at their mother
sitting there, almost jaunty; suited, hatted, and
gloved; hearing that she was going on a journey
but would see them all sooner than soon, with a
double present for each one who had been a little
lady or gentleman.

Out of the window I could see across the street
men watching from the gallery of Gaylord's sad-
dlery, and I knew that someone had recognized
Lutie Brewton. Then there were quick steps in my
outer office, and Myra Netherwood, tall and gray-
haired, an excited look on her dignified face, was
there.

" Doctor, they tell me — " she began. " Lutie! "
And they were in each other's arms.

Out in the plaza I heard the rattle of my phaeton's wheels from the livery stable.

"You comin', doc? " called the messenger from
the next county.

I moved to finish packing my doctor bag.

" I've got to make a little call — on a sick man,"
I told Lutie with my back turned. " I know you'll
want to be with Mrs. Netherwood. I'll come over as
soon as I get in."

I tried to put it as if it were only a near-by
nester patient, but I knew when I turned, by the
same pale branch whipsawing again in the stream

of blood at her throat, that her sensitive mind had
guessed where I was going. And all the long trail
down into the South Prairie country, while the
rancher who had ridden all night dozed beside me,
I could see in the endless heat waves two unforgettable looks in Lutie Brewton's brilliant dark eyes.
One of them was when she had seen on the wall the
framed photograph of my uncle, an old man, a
great frame without flesh, sitting in his buggy,
holding the reins of his pair of sorrels. The other
look she had given me when I left. It concerned
nothing of this world, only a small boy in a long
nightgown and tousled hair white in the candle-
light of a world that had vanished like last year's
snows.

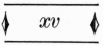

xv

I⊤ was Sunday morning when my horses' shoes splashed silently back again in the floury brown dust of Salt Fork streets. The wooden shutters were up on mercantile houses, the doors of business places closed, and that strange Sabbath stillness hung over everything as if these whitewashed galleries and brown adobe walls had not heard only yesterday the untamed roar of dance hall and six-

shooter or seen of an early morning the dregs of
the wild night before swinging silently from tree
and water-tower.

Even when I turned in my team at Dagget's
livery stable, it was Sunday there among the peacefully munching horses in their stalls. But all the
while I drew my straight razor above the wooden
wash-stand in my room and while I made my way
across the plaza with the Spanish bells from the
thick-walled adobe church clanging in my ears, I
dreaded meeting Lutie Brewton.

Then I knocked on the Netherwood door, pan-
eled and grained, with a kind of knob I seldom see
any more, and Lutie Brewton opened it herself,
slender and rigidly erect as I had ever remembered
her. Only the plumed hat looked as if it were bear-
ing down too hard on that fragile head and throat,
and the eyes in the white face burned with a high
fever.

" Don't tell me anything — yet, Hal! " she said.
" Just take me to mass. Myra can't go. And I don't
want to be stared at alone."

My uncle and I seldom went to church. And I
would have given a great deal to escape it this
morning. I had never been out with Lutie Brewton before when the nearness of other people had
not been the stimulus for the most animated con-

versation to her companion. But today the only
emotion at their approach was the tightening of
her arm in mine as it had that day so long ago when
together we had passed the murdered teamster
lying in the straw of his wagon with a bandanna
over his face.

Once we were sitting in the dim church, with the
candles mystically winking and the dull red of
the sanctuary light glowing in the dark cave of the
altar, it was as if she no longer knew I was there.
The click of her beads was strangely like the click
of six-shooters, and the sibilants of her lips like
those of the wind drawing through rusty barbed
wire and yerba de vibora. The whitewashed walls of
the church kept passing away like mist, and instead
of the altar, there in front of me was the barren
South Prairie as I had driven through it the last
several days, naked in the pitiless Southwestern
sunlight, with discouraged nester families watching my phaeton from the doors of occupied dugouts and the doors of the empty houses half-fallen
from their hinges. I saw plows rusting and gaunt
horses standing motionless where there had once
been grass. And the sand still drifted along the
crazy pattern of abandoned fence-posts.

And at the end of the journey wounded men
stupefied with whisky lay half-undressed under a

leafless, sapless apple tree. A fresh mound of earth
dried and cracked in the sun like a giant adobe
brick. And I knew that around a rough circle of
sand hills, hidden men with rifles watched the
cañada where a deserted nester's shack stared sul-
lenly from its empty windows.

Chamberlain had not yet arrived, and we had
no idea then that he never expected to come, that
even at this hour he was boarding a train for Santa
Fe on some unnamed judicial business. And after
the sun went down and a horse's hoofs sounded
on the trail, we thought it was the judge or news of
the judge at last, even when the sound told us there
was no buggy. Then as it drew closer through the
Western twilight that tonight hung almost red
over the land, there was something familiar about
the rider hunched on the saddle of a weary, raw-
boned roan with lathered shoulders.

" It's the old Colonel," someone muttered after
a little.

The men stared at each other and back at the
apparition. And now I could make out clearly
enough the unmistakable figure of my uncle on his
favorite, silver-horned saddle, a weary old man in
a gray broadcloth coat too large for his shrunken
girth and shoulders, unarmed, his coat-tails

spreading behind the cantle, his trousers tucked into boots brown with dust. Who had told him about Brock I had no idea, but he had ridden a direct line across the country from the Cross B, over malpais and timbered ridges where no buggy trail ran. His roan was caked with mud far above the knees where he had plainly forded the treacherous Puerco, and the Navajo blanket protruding from the saddle was dark with sweat.

He halted beside us presently, his great head with its long gray mustaches forward on the soiled linen of his chest. His burned-out eyes seemed to peer at us from far back in his head where life had taken a final stand. And if there was a sign of recognition for any of us, I didn't see it, and for all the attention he showed me, I might have been a stranger instead of Brewton flesh and blood.

" Where's Brock? " was all he asked.

The men stirred uncomfortably. One of them indicated the cañada. For several moments the old eyes peered at the deserted squalid shack, a symbol of all that he hated and that had brought him tragedy and pain. Then the gray wrinkled knees nudged his mount; his old fingers, no more than bone, veins, and skin, twitched the reins, and the tired roan started.

The sheriff caught the bridle.

" You can't go down there," he said. " Not till Judge Chamberlain comes."

For a little it seemed that my uncle didn't understand him, as if it took a long time for that name to penetrate some inner room of his being where the embers of life still glowed. Then he raised his shaggy head in a semblance of that old untamed gesture of a mossy-horned lead steer smelling wolves or water. I had never seen him lift it so slowly, but when the face came up, I saw with a feeling for which there are no words that somewhere in that old Indian-fighter frame still remained the breeding-place of the whirlwind and thunderbolt. Already the hate had begun to pour from his pitch-black eyes, and his face was written again with all those unforgettable black lines of insolent, almost dissolute, will and ruthlessness.

A dozen sheriffs could not have held him now, and none of us tried it, or said anything as we watched him, rigidly erect in the saddle, his right arm held stiffly down against his side with his thumb at the cantle edge as was his custom from army days, ride down alone into the cañada where a low deadly voice we could barely hear hailed him from the nester's shack, warning him he would never give himself up alive for trial, that the old man wasn't his father anyway, and that if he came any closer, he would drop both horse and rider in the trail.

No answer came from my uncle, and the only change in that lone, riding figure was that he seemed to tower in his stirrups so that two hundred yards away, with his back turned, I felt that time had leaped back twenty years, that the clumps of rattlesnake weed melting into each other on the horizon were solid green range, and I might almost see a wave of antelope, rusty as with kelp, rising and falling over my uncle's sea of grass.

He had been in the shack only a few minutes when he was outside ordering me in his old-time thunder to come. When I got there, an unshaven man sat propped up against the wall with rifle and pistol on the floor beside him, mocking and grimacing at me, his yellow hair curling like a child's. And all the time my hand wanted to shake as I tried in the dim light from the doorway to stop the bleeding from a wound in his lung, and while my uncle stood there with tortured stolidity, Brock lay on the dirty floor, paying no attention to my command to be quiet, jibing and mimicking me, calling me a horse doctor, begging tobacco and smoking cigarettes, bantering about Jimmy and Tom Mille-deaux and coaxing me to say nice things about him to Sarah Beth, so that no one, not even the sheriff, standing silent and listening some feet beyond the door, could help being won over to him now.

And in the firelight that evening, when he couldn't talk any more and there was no sound but the yapping of the coyotes, I thought I saw his sardonic blue eyes pointing to something behind me. The shack had been systematically riddled with lead by the posse until it was almost a sieve. Only one conspicuous place on the four walls remained untouched by bullets, and I found now that he was derisively drawing my attention to what hung pasted by unknown hands to the center of this spot, a faded, Christmas newspaper print of Christ in the manger, with the well-known words: " Peace on Earth, Good Will toward Men."

The ringing of a bell somewhere and the rising and dipping of the congregation brought the whitewashed walls of the church back again with Lutie Brewton beside me. And when I looked about I was aware now that most of the people around us must have already heard of what had happened on the South Prairie. Their stares at Lutie Brewton carried a questioning as if they were not so sure but that yesterday they had wronged her. Her sensitive mind seemed to feel and respond to their new respect, and when the services were over, I thought she seemed to be again that clear pure flame burning from something far more precious than tallow.

When she went out she lifted her veil and smiled gently to the little Mexican girls admiring her as they kept dipping their knees at aisle and door, and spoke, as she had in the old days, to a sightless, black-shawled Mexican, now an old woman known as La Ciega. The latter, I am sure, had never understood one of Lutie Brewton's sparkling English sentences, although a look had always come into her blind, wrinkled face as if she had talked to someone who had seen the Blessed Virgin.

But today at the sound of that charming, unmistakable voice she had not heard for fifteen years, La Ciega let go of her rebozo and reached out to the speaker, and her hands were tight lumps of brown copper against Lutie Brewton's white slender ones.

" *Ay de mi, señora!* " she began, and poured out a stream of Spanish from one woman to another.

Lutie stood there delicately responsive and sympathetic, glancing questioningly to me. But when, without translating any of it, I tried to urge her quietly on, she turned attentively to a Mexican youth who rolled barrels and pulled square nails in John Kingman's warehouse.

" What does the blind woman say? "

" She say," the boy said, arching his back with pride to be speaking to Mrs. Brewton in front of everybody, " She say she have a boy too who is kill by a bullet. She said thank to God her boy and your boy don't suffer any more."

" Yes," Lutie Brewton said, drawing in her breath. " Yes, thank her for me."

She was erect again and very white as she took my arm and went on, steadily clearing the multi-colored stream of churchgoers still flowing and eddying out of the ancient thick-walled church.

" Now I am ready to go to the ranch, Hal," she said. " Will you have someone from Dagget's livery drive me? "

" I wouldn't go until the funeral, Lutie? " I begged her in a low voice.

The plumes of her hat were suddenly and rigidly higher.

" May I go right away this morning, Hal, please! " she asked, and I found that her clearly modulated voice impelled me toward the livery stable as effectively as twenty years ago it had turned rough men about and whipped off their hats until the aisle had opened for us into the crowded Salt Fork county courthouse.

A hundred times since she had gone away I had pictured Lutie Brewton coming back to the

Cross B. And in my thoughts I was always there, feeling that extraordinary, quickening emotion just the sight of her had always called up in me. But today the old ranch house was the last place on earth I wanted to go with Lutie Brewton. And all the way to the livery stable I could see my uncle's eyes; flaming, terrible eyes as I had seen them in the South Prairie country only yesterday.

Frank Dagget gave me a queer look when I asked him for a pair of fresh horses in my phaeton to drive to the Cross B. And I knew he had guessed who was going with me, for he lifted his best black harness from the long pins, laid it on the back of his fastest team, and said that the boxing of one of the wheels of my old dusty phaeton was loose and he would give me today the fine green-seated buggy he had only last week unloaded from the railroad. And before he let me go, he combed again the manes and tails of his team and flecked the fine particles of dust from shiny black spokes, leather dash and whipstock.

" Is she well? " he asked, not looking at me.

" I think so," I said.

" It takes spunk to go to the old Colonel now," he said as I climbed into the buggy. " But then she always had it."

There are days in our Southwestern country

that people call brassy but should be called steel. The sun beats down with a merciless white fire until the cloudless sky is scarcely blue but rather like the blade of a knife that for days has been ground to the stone. And all day it cuts open the breathing body of the prairie and lays its bones dead and bare in the pitiless glare before you.

It was such a morning I drove out of the wide front doors of the livery, and I felt for Lutie Brewton and how she would flinch. But I had no need to. Although Myra Netherwood in a silk wrapper gave me an anguished glance, Lutie Brewton came out of her room delicate and fragile but up and never to be turned back now, showing me the valises to carry to the buggy as if she had been away from the ranch no more than to come to town and would find everything on her return as she had left it a few days before. She gave little sign that the townspeople watched her as we drove away, and once we had reached the prairie, she kept her face turned from all the nester sores and scars, talking in a low incessant voice, as if she could not halt if she wished. But although I listened for any touch here or there that would reveal the pattern of her hidden years, I knew no more afterwards than before which of the stories of those who said they had seen her was the true one.

Only at dusk when, after pushing the team, we saw the ranch buildings and trees swimming ahead of us like an oasis in a purple desert, was she silent. And she didn't speak again until we had driven through the wall of cottonwoods and tamarisks she herself had had planted and had stopped by the dark familiar walls of the ranch house, dimly lighted by a lantern slung from a hook on the wide front gallery.

I learned that my uncle had not yet returned from the South Prairie, from where he was expected an hour or two ahead of the wagon. But under the candles that Lutie Brewton went about lighting, the whole house was grimly eloquent with his presence; his implacable, sweated gun belt hanging from its accustomed corner of the pine settee in the hall; his wrinkled, unyielding boots standing along the wall in the big front bedroom where Lutie directed me to set down her valises; the inflexible shape of his pipes lying about; and the fierce spartan barrenness of everything.

I wished to God that Jimmy might come in from somewhere in the cedar country, where, they told me, they had sent a rider with the news. As the evening went on, there was no sign of him. But after an hour the older headquarters hands who had known Mrs. Brewton moved in a body from the bunkhouse to greet her and pay their respects, lining up on the front gallery and pushing the foreman first, all grave and embarrassed, ceremoniously shaven and in clean shirts, holding their hats in their hands, scraping the high heels of their boots, feeling tremendously sorry for her about Brock and all that had happened before and all that might happen when the old Colonel came home, but the farthermost notion from their minds that of expressing a word of it.

Soberly each one spoke as he shook hands.

" Nice day, Miz Brewton."

" You have a nice trip from town, Miz Brewton? "

" Find the road pretty fair, Miz Brewton? "

And after that they said little enough, just stood around respectfully until such a time should elapse that it would be fitting for them to go. What few remarks they managed to make they chose with extreme care, avoiding anything that might assume that Brock had ever lived or died or that she had gone away. And all the while Lutie Brewton, her face very pale against her dark hair, tried to make them less uncomfortable, cross-stitching and embroidering their simplest subjects, picking up in her white fingers the most ordinary sentiment spoken with sawdust and awkwardness, and breathing upon it till it grew golden and exciting and important so that the others looked with surprise at the original speaker for having uttered it.

And when the time they waited for had elapsed, it was as hard for them to go as it had been to come. Once or twice I thought a cowhand near the door lifted his head to listen. Then even without ears I would have known by the way they stiffened and their features flattened into leather that a step had sounded on the front gallery. And when I looked up, my uncle was towering in the doorway, a picture struck violently on my brain so that today he still seems to be standing there, an untamed shape in the shadows, charged with turbulent will and power, his deep eyes burning with orange flames at what they glimpsed in the wide hallway.

When I glanced back, the cowhands were solemnly taking their leave, mumbling: " Good night, Miz Brewton," going as they came, in single shuffling file, until at last Lutie Brewton stood there alone, a slight, almost frail, feminine figure, rooted against the approaching storm.

My uncle came forward slowly, still a kind of rude king in his tailed gray broadcloth, and when he was under the lights I could see that the forked veins stood out in his neck as he bowed over her hand, asking with unfailing courtesy about her health. But his furrowed face was a mask and his voice granite, and I knew that while all the others in Salt Fork county might tactfully shy from the subject where she had been all these years and what she had been doing, my uncle now would not for a moment avoid it.

And I think Lutie Brewton knew it, too, and resolved in her mind that she would never be cross-examined and compelled to explain as if she were a child, and it only made her eyes more brilliant and tilted back her fragile head piled with its black hair at a gallant, almost defiant angle, while she threw herself not into her old gayety but a grave and desperate incoherence, asking about his welfare, and where was Jimmy, and telling him that Myra had shown her Jimmy's and Sarah Beth's photographs, and mustn't he be terribly tired from his long ride, and couldn't she get something for him to eat and drink? And when my uncle's eyes grew darker with dammed-back questions, she spoke the faster, and her face became very thin and intense ivory, faintly streaked and stained as if by the blood of the creature that had borne it.

Until at last I couldn't bear it any longer and, while my uncle's eyes flared at me, I leaped to my feet and begged her to make us some coffee or rouse the cook to build a fire. Certainly I expected her to seize the chance to leave the room, but she only stood there with her face higher and cut finer, and an indecipherable look in her feverish eyes, till I was the one who escaped, bolting to the bunk-house, where I found the hands up far beyond their bedtime, smoking, talking in low tones, waiting for the wagon.

When an hour or two later I went stiffly back across the front gallery, some chemical change had taken place in those ancient walls. The air of the massive old ranch house hung with the elusive scent of violets high on the peaceful fumes of cigar smoke. In the wide hall the brightly colored Navajo rugs had been laid again over the pine settees. A great white cloth hung low from the heavy dining-table set with four places for tomorrow's breakfast. And the parlor I could see was swept and dusted in readiness for the coming visitor who had not been home for many a day. There were fresh doilies on the marble-top tables and clean tidies on the chair backs. The piano still stood closed, but the tall ornamental brass floor-lamp had been lighted, and the blue, entwined flowers bloomed again on the hand-painted china shade.

Then my uncle, who had been sitting quietly on a horsehair armchair, raised his head in that undy-ing gesture of a wild stallion, his half-smoked cigar held suddenly motionless in his hand. Through the door to the front bedroom I saw Lutie Brewton stand perfectly still while she clutched folded clean sheets in her bare white arms. After a moment, far away on the lonely trail under the Southwestern stars I could hear the tolling rumble of the approaching wagon.

There is little more to tell except that the last time I was back the stone my uncle raised was still standing near the broken walls of the old ranch house.

" Brock Brewton, son of James B. and Lutie C. Brewton," it is carved in unequivocal letters that all who ride may read.

I remember very well the first time I saw it. In Salt Fork, people were still divided about Brock and where Mrs. Brewton had been. I was aware that Lutie Brewton herself would never reveal the truth to any of them, perhaps never to me. This particular day she and Sarah Beth, who was home for a month, had driven in the Colonel's pole buggy to the Bar 44. My uncle was sitting on the ranch-house gallery from where he could see the stone. And from what he said to me while his eyes rested on it, his motives were clear to me at last as a + B brand.

" Have you noticed how young she still looks,

Hal? " he asked, filling his chair again with that iron dignity and pride I remembered as a boy. " It was a hard thing for a lady to go through. But she's one in a thousand, Hal. No one else will ever be like her." And his deeply lined face warmed like the late afternoon sun touching and mellowing the rugged western slope of a shaggy old mountain.

This book is composed in Linotype " Scotch ". This style of type came into fashion in England and the United States by way of fonts cast at the foundry of Alex. Wilson & Son at Glasgow in 1833. It was a style of letter that echoed the " classical " taste of the time, and would seem to have been inspired by the kind of letter-shapes that result when you cut lettering on a copper plate with a graver — just as visiting-cards are cut now. It is more precise and *vertical* in character than the " old style " types (such as Caslon) that it displaced.

The book was designed by W. A. Dwiggins.